4 | Lemons on a plate...(an alter-ego speaks)

LEMONS ON A PLATE

ON A

PLATE

(an alter-ego speaks)

VOLUME 1

A NOVEL BY

PAT BLACK

Lemons on a plate...
(*an alter-ego speaks*)

VOLUME I

a novel by

PAT BLACK

Designed by Pat Black Productions

ISBN 978-1-5136-3910-9

To my 2.

**Lemons on a plate...
(an alter-ego speaks)**

"The plate represents the universe. The lemons are what's in it. That is all."

-Below Thought-

10 | Lemons on a plate...(an alter-ego speaks)

Just call me Tom, or Kathy, or even fish. The designation, label, or title put on me is simply a marker or signpost there used for the purpose of identifying me, versus the one I seek to represent in these words. It is imperative that I, the narrator, am not important here; I bring no significant role to this reading. I only bring thought and emotion to the table and the only reason I call myself "I" is for you, the reader, to understand me in what is contemplated as language; in this case, the English language.

Ken, though, is the one I represent. He is the human in which the following words will tell of, not in an analytical or superficial way, or with intent to define, but in a simplistic way that these words, the words of the human form, allow. To put it bluntly, as the humanoid would verse, I am the alter-ego of Ken Modd, or Colonel Kenneth James Modd, as he would willingly title himself.

You see, reader, this all came about a few months ago when Barron Desulfer, an esteemed literature professor began writing again. Through chance, Ken Modd found Barron and a professional relationship began. Ken called on the poor and desperate "down on his luck" humanoid Barron to be the central navigator, author, and writer of the details of a military and civilian career that seemed important enough to Ken to desire a need for publication into an autobiography. Ken's ego sought fame and fortune from the project, but I, his altered state of consciousness, sought peace and refuge.

As an altered state, I have no concept of what "time" is, so perhaps 'dimension-time' is more appropriate; but for the purposes of yielding to the status quo of the humanoid practice, I will use "time". Though I can easily discuss ego and spiritual concepts in a fundamental way here, it may be suitable for a different forum. I will initially use terms that better suit me, such as humanoid and transformation, but I will progress into human terminology gradually in the writings. For you, reader, it is essential to pay particular attention to the dates; follow them closely.

Understand here, too, that I am void of the necessary writing ability to create a tale or story; I am not keen to using writing language that is created with literary proficiency under the guise of editorial guidelines. I have no care what one thinks of with regard to my editorial and publishing take on these matters. I am simply, without cause or effort, approaching you, reader, to gain an understanding of a man's perspective on things without his own input. I, as the altered state of Ken Modd's consciousness, will guide you through the difficult transgressions that lie ahead.

Everything you see as statements in italics will be my non-humanoid input or guidance. It is merely a pointer for us two to walk, side-by-side, in this compelling series of words and happenings before us.

Chapter one starts with the words of Barron, as written in his own personal journal…

I.

27th of November

I live in a bridge tender shack. It is rife with spider webs and brown dust; at times I cannot distinguish one from the other. The old bridge, a reticulated and narrow object, used to support itself over the muddy water of the waterway but now the waterway has dried up to the point where it can no longer be identified as an old waterway; filled with cattails, swamp grass, and new trees. And the only thing you can see from a distance-if you care to look that far, hidden within the cattails, swamp grass, and new trees-is the thin, rusty ladder going up to the bridge tender shack.

The old broken cedar door that enters the shack has been worked on many times by quick-witted carpenters who have spent time there. The brass that makes up its hinges and hardware has become soft and brittle; the lower hinge is a tongue from an old steel-toed boot that rests near the steps, filled with dirt, weeds, and a single small yellow flower that grew by accident. The thin pane glass that an old bridge tender once polished is gnarled and cracked; only duct tape holds it together; I imagine that is old, too.

Not much longer than eight feet, the only room is narrow and lanky with a low, flat ceiling. A big couch takes up all of one wall and much of the floor area; I use it for sitting, eating, and sleeping. Next to it is a fluted coal oil lamp that was left behind after only a single or two uses; the black soot that stays permanent on the glass hadn't even reached the top of the cylinder. On the other wall, decrepit and chipped, is a frame with a photo of me getting an award; it's an old relic I cherish. And of course, there is the tall one-man round table teeter-tottering on two rusty sign posts held together, back-to-back, with two wing-nut bolts; it is where I spend most of my days in this shack-writing; there are folded up dusty napkins under the feet that keep it sturdy and balanced. There is nothing else inside the place but a threadbare, dirty pillow without a pillowcase, broken chips of cedar used for heating the outside fire, and old bridge tender records yellowed and folded neatly by someone other than me in a dusty box on the floor down to the left by the lamp.

On the frail wooden porch just outside there is a small framed closet with no door. It is where I keep my whiskey bottles. Oh, to correct myself-where I previously kept my whiskey bottles! I am sober now and have been for many months. The diabolical demons of drug and alcohol abuse that ran havoc over me and controlled my life no longer do.

13th of January

Today I placed an ad on the corkboard at the family grocery store where I sweep and mop the floors to make a few dollars; it is a far cry from the six-figure income I earned as a professor at the University. The ad, penned on a piece of crinkled brown paper bag, like the one you hold a beer in to keep it cold and the frost off of your hands, simply tells that I am a successful writer seeking my next project.

The advertisement doesn't say that I had four acknowledged and successful books in my early days. Nor does it say that I was a very pronounced literature professor with seven scholar articles, two invitations to Cambridge, and runner-up of the Hemingway Award for achievement.

It doesn't say that the publishing company that proclaimed my four books set forward a pattern of deceit, declared bankruptcy, and pirated all of my future earnings. Nor does the ad utter that the University fired me after seventeen years of gainful occupation; and they broke off paying my pension two years after that!

The ad on the small brown crinkled paper doesn't say that only four teeth remain in my mouth (the methamphetamine does that to one); or that half of my stomach has been removed because of alcohol abuse-well-one won't read that on the advertisement either. How hideous and ghastly such an ad would read!

It may seem, on the surface, casual that I write, but the truth of the matter is, I continue to compose words not because it is my beloved pastime or I am devoured in boredom, nor am I distracted from life, and I am much too set in my ways to have a pastime or hobby. No, I am adamant about representing the reason I write; there is a rational one; it is exclusively a matter of me losing my memory (the drugs were entirely culpable).

Though I do not have enough evidence of this, I can only imagine that when the memory has completely diminished and is non-existent, the details will only reemerge through these writings, editorials, and brief comments. In this thousand-page journal, this collective array of talk that I have kept for the past thirty-one years, one would find a great measure of humor, a little blasphemy, and stalwart discussions on religion, politics, and the abstraction of a poor soul, wandering in life and residing in a bridge tender shack rife with spiders and brown dust; at times the two indistinguishable from each other. One would find a man's general colloquy with himself, both enquiring and rebutting; often providing his own answer to his own question. I find this titillating and provoking at best! But the loss of my memory does disturb me to a great degree and I find no humor in it. In fact, if I were not to have a love for writing-an indescribable feeling of relief and comfort that the soul rarely feels-when I write, then I would find the entire act of writing to be of high maintenance, burdensome, and time-consuming.

I have a pet peeve-it is a singular annoyance; there are not many critical decrees that I create for myself, but this is one-I never return to read my writing; it is simply not meaningful to do so. If my memory slips me about a particular practical matter, then, and *only* then, will I return to see what time my appointment is or who I am supposed to meet or to recollect something.

That is all. There is no use in living a repetitious, long-winded life where events are played out repeatedly; time must move forward.

II.

18th of January

Today two people affixed a request to speak with me onto the brown paper advertisement in which I attached to the corkboard at the grocery store. I walked outside to the payphone and called the first one; after five minutes of conversation, it became evident, only then, that it was a prankster; a lonely old man with nothing better to do with his time. In all of this mischievousness, I found no humor in it; the rascal simply wasted my time and half the change in my pocket. I wished him no ill will, though. We are all lost and lonely in this world, at one time or another; that is what we are taught to believe.

Then, without haste, I dialed the second one. After a long series of rings someone answered. "Hello, this is Colonel Modd." The loud-voiced man introduced himself. After I gave my lucid, yet short introduction, he continued. "I'm a highly commended military officer- U.S. Army, of course- who's fought in six wars and I'm seeking someone to write my autobiography. I look to leave a legacy behind and am in search of a leader with your credentials, professor." At this moment, I could not help but become flush as he spoke so ardent to me, with high regard. We held a dialogue for about ten minutes and the conversation concluded with the details of his home address. After the conversation I stood in silence, in a mannered unbelief. "Could it be that finally the course of my life is about to change?" I thought with little skepticism.

I looked at the Colonel's address once again and taped it to the wall next to my framed award. His home is a considerable distance from here and taxi fare is expected to be lavish. I must do an accounting of my funds, dear book.

It is arranged for us to meet in a fortnight; I do not know what I will do with myself for two weeks, but preparedness must be of primary importance, for this could be the biggest break-some hope that I need-and haven't had, in years.

22nd of January

I acquired an old tweed jacket outside of the drug store today in the bright cool morning, while I stood and stared at the sun. I shared with the old man (Mr. Zinglinger) the details of my potential opportunity and he was overjoyed to offer a jacket that had rested in his closet for some time. It was a little tight, a bit cavalier, and the left side elbow patch needed sewing, so I managed it. I cannot wonder, though, if the Colonel will notice the white string sewn onto the brown canvas patch; those military types, they observe everything. The penny loafers remain two sizes too small and still hurt my toes at times; I thought wearing them over the past few months would stretch them out some but that hasn't happened, and probably won't. I contemplated asking the old man (Mr. Zinglinger) for a pair, just to wear for the trip, but in my embarrassment and indebtedness, decided against it.

I cannot apprehend, beforehand, the nature of what Colonel Modd's assumptions and expectancies will be. Perhaps his perceptive and astute practice as a military expert will yield admirable accounts that I can compose with immense thought and provocation; perhaps they will be memoirs of strife and hostility so agonizing, so austere, that I will personally succumb to the numbing effects of the sensitivity of war, and become paralyzed by its ramifications. Oh, how silly to reek in such ambiguous thought with over a week before our meeting. Without clarity, I would only drive myself into an asylum by thinking in such way; and if they discovered that my illness required me to write almost everything down, then, with much certainty, I would be placed underneath the asylum and fed wood chips!

What is more important to think of, with open optimism, is what I will do with the earnings from the writings. Oh, there are many things to think of; the teeth that so perilously trouble me with discomfort each day-such a vehement pain-or the atrocious living conditions that betray me inwardly-living in such squalor-or the dreary and oft questionable future that lay before me. How could man live in such penny-pinching ways in this day and age? So stingy so as not even eat or keep one's self warm when it is cold out. Undeniably, if God says the same, this will be the portal to something more aligned with my intentions of yesteryears, when prosperity and good luck reigned upon me. Perhaps I would be so fortunate to drive a car again and take myself to places instead of relying on taxicabs and neighbors. It would be so inviting to visit the mountains or even the beach or even long-lost colleagues not seen in decades.

11106 Bradford Drive in Heighton Park; one of the more affluent expanses of the city; million-dollar homes with tall roofs and white fences; fancy Jaguars surging past. I just know that the tides will turn; Colonel Modd will be generous to me; oh, how I feel this! He will be a stepping-stone for me, a delightful stepping-stone that will turn up possibility after possibility; my faith and belief shall not deny me.

05th of February, morning

My nerves are cracking like thunder on a lake. I am desperate to attain the magical ways of a magician and turn this day into tomorrow; for tomorrow is the day I await with such apprehensive anticipation. I have lay here, in this rickety shack with low ceilings, and stared at them until they appeared so close to my face, conceivably ready to dance or kiss. Or, maybe it has been the dozens of pages of notes I have written about my anxiety over this waiting that has kept me preoccupied in the time that has passed. I do not know. I am adrift of an answer to this beleaguered inquisition. Tomorrow will come; it will arrive by the grace of God. I need not place resistance on the time that exists; it passes too quickly as it is.

In the meantime, I have thought of my beloved parents; each time I submerse myself in a writing sojourn they retain a measured presence in my mind. Good people who, too, were well versed and educated in the ways of literature; they were simple and frugal. When I was two, we left the states and relocated to Finland for a few years; they studied Russian literature and taught at local universities while I stayed home and was tutored by a young Fin girl. At eight we moved to London; to the rat holes of the suburbs of the bustling city. They taught English at local schoolhouses and I worked in meager part-time jobs while finishing my primary education. I did not like London very much at the time, as I felt it to be too harsh and colonized; getting around was not easy, costs were very high, and the people were oft cliquish. But I do like it some now, that is, the last time I visited, about ten years ago. Oh, how I miss my beloved parents and I cannot conceive how troubling and petulant a human would be by losing such wonderful memories of one's family. I do not know, now at this point in my life-I cannot remember-if I have all of the memories of my family, or if only half have been lost.

05th of February, evening

I woke up from the couch from my afternoon nap groggy. There were no crazy dreams or arthritic joints giving me pain today; just didn't rest well.

I sat across the small wobbly table from a book; I didn't even recognize it; not it's form, not its color, or the words of the title. The tears hung around the bottom edges of my eyes, not even brazen enough to fall. I cannot believe a book that I have written in for over three decades, and I do not remember it for a brief lapse of time.
That is the sad part, oh book. And with everything there is a dichotomy that exists; I remembered you,

easily, when I opened the cover and began to read the words. It all came back to me, as though it had never left.

Another apperception of mine today was that I had a face-to-face with the one who steal memories. How silly, but I recognized it for the first time in decades. It scares me to know that one day when my memory fades out like that, I may meander deep enough in memory loss to not ever recapture your words again, oh book.

When I began writing the book, "The Distance Between Fenceposts", I was engulfed with work and a second wife who was not well, and my alcoholism that was just beginning to come to light. And so, my life was cluttered and strewn with so much. I seemed to be going somewhere in my career, but slowly; trickling along. Someone pointed out to me that I should become more organized. And so, I did.

I threw away seven different wire-bound notebooks, filled with two years of essays, critical writing, notes, computations, comments, and the like; copied half, and threw the other half away, really. I began to think how I would organize my writing, notes, and the other things simply to get rid of the clutter in my life. It was chaos that was completely unnecessary, and at times drove me mad.

An idea in a bookstore seemed perfect; a massive journal with hardback, nylon-bound covers, able to be used and abused from the hardships of opening and closing, with dirty hands often; the stress on the paper from the pen pressed too hard from a few moments anger, and the ebb and flow of being the center of attention and constantly handled.

Everything I wrote went into the journal; this journal right in front of me, and you *yourself*, oh book, I add with such peculiarity. Political stories, critical thoughts on writing, opportunities and threats, too. There were personal love letters to and from, daily training notes, a contact list, and, within the last ten years, as my memory has receded, a daily journal.

Storing you in the dresser drawer, hidden away, worked fine for the first and second year after the diagnosis, but, as it got worse, I noticed, the dates between writings got progressively longer and longer, and I was ostensibly writing less. But now, great friend, I keep you on the back of the toilet.

Every political speech given by Fidel Castro is copied in this journal. The writings that excited me most, my treasures that tell of a certain ballerina dancing for sixteen years, are in this book. Life as it be in other places fills a bulk of the stiff white pages, too; stories of simple life in the Middle East, food tasting in the America's, and aphrodisiacal moments in India can be found; no long-winded writing, just quick observances.

Reader, today the humanoid Barron (you have been reading the words of his personal journal) meets Colonel Ken Modd. His first impression will be cemented into his mind and remain there as the most significant encounter of his life; it will provide him with an energy that will have enduring effect. He reaches out to Ken with amazing impartiality and broad-mindedness and arrives with no judgment. He is fully ready to take the wisdom and success of his own life's work and study to create a phenomenal masterpiece, based on another man's life events.

I.

06th of February

Ah, what a dazzling man I have finally had the pleasure to meet-Colonel Kenneth James Modd! I did not think, by my own unfettered anxiety, that I would be able to march up the concrete walkway, pass the colorful and unyielding tall tulips, stand politely with my head high, and ring the doorbell this morning, much less ensconce myself in beautiful accommodations to receive such a fine welcome and inevitably listen attentively to the Colonel's animus. I did so, though, without self-scrutiny or unlevel headedness, and, in some time, the impatience and discomfiture went away, not to return and reveal itself again.

I did not expect the Colonel to be an appalling, ill-statured man of few words, and certainly he wasn't. After I rang the doorbell I followed his shadow getting closer and closer to the entrance door. The six-foot statue looked down at me standing at the bottom step of the landing, timid as a young child with lemonade for sale. He had a fresh haircut, not a high and tight Marine cut where everything below the crown of the head is shaved, but more like a short business mans haircut. His back was wide, his shoulders broad, and his calves were thick; I presume such legs are acquired from years of harsh, non-stop road marches. He assuredly fit the build of a military man.

Each room of the immense home was embellished with fine furnishings; most undoubtedly from other places in the world. Ornate stone, large boulders, and thin, long rectangular mirrors could be seen throughout the expansive open living and dining areas.

Though I am unrefined in the recognition and cultivation of international art, each one of the pieces that shroud the walls and engross the rooms summons a magnificent story and embodies a level of eminence. I could only imagine, as I stared furiously, that at the time each piece was purchased, it was done so in a formidable and deliberate manner, with much contemplation. Placing such romantic and evolutionary pieces in their respective places within the home, too, must have been done with much thought.

What it all means seems to lead in a single direction. The Colonel has been blessed by his accomplishments and devotion and he exemplifies eloquence and orderliness at every turn; I levy by his surroundings. His life's journey, one in which I will soon set sail to study, analyze, comprehend exceptionally, pen into words and distribute to the world, I am certain, has been distinguished and commendable!

The two large white Siamese cats sprinting, hopping, and resting on the white couches in the large living area presented humor at times and at other times became objects to evaluate as the Colonel answered the phone or prepared tea in the kitchen for our discussion. It was a delicious licorice tea with some herbs sprinkled on top; not too strong or sweet, not too bitter; one of Middle Eastern decent, I can infer.

Characterizing his life as "a wholesome, decorated, and prophetic journey", the Colonel gave me every reason to be confidant that an unmeasured success waits inescapably for me. At one point this morning, during a conversation about military readiness, I drifted off into reflection of a visit to the dentist. I imagined that I sat there and he held out in front of my face a menu; I pointed out what services I wished for and instructed him to proceed. Of course, this little daydream was interrupted when one of the cats-the one with the small brown spot on his face- pounced onto my lap, jumped wildly, and left long strands of hair on my pants. Oh, how I giggled out loud! The interruption allowed the Colonel to briefly take his mind off our conversation to pick up the animal, and too, allowed me to catch up with the conversation as he, an avid gentleman, reverted backwards in dialogue some as a result of the cat's mischievous misgivings of sort, and my wandering off to other thoughts.

I was confounded, yet comfortable to learn, oh book, that Colonel Modd had performed due diligence on my professorship at the University as well as the books in which I wrote. His research was proficient and thorough and he knew much about me. He was impressed with my work, giddy of my success, and markedly sad about the way I was fired without cause. "Professor, your work was rich and prolific. Those who let you go left behind literary triumphs that will never be realized or known. There is no guess as to what could have materialized in such a vested career." I felt that I blushed and placed my hand on my hot face. What a compliment! I thought silently, but almost out loud. In the face of it all, though, I remained calm, minded my manners, and continued to take notes of his expectations and requests, all the while, deep inside, erupting with jubilance.

As the conversation neared its end, the Colonel stood up with his arms wide open and his hands unclasped and he told me, "The most important rule I have, Mr. Barron, is that by no means whatsoever do I want to read the autobiography before it's been completed; I don't want to waste precious time in the minutia of it all; the fiddle-faddle, if you will." He smiled as he stated to me that he took this word 'fiddle-faddle' directly from me; that I had used it before in one of my books. He continued. "I do not have much time, nor capacity to attribute to this endeavor; the time I spend with you interviewing me will be more than sufficient and we will achieve considerable success through our communications. You'll come to me when it's written and we'll discuss matters then." I took this rule to heart, making sure to write it down as I thought of my ailing memory, and nodded with great concentration, as my mind remained lingering on the 'fiddle-faddle' word and its origin in my other book.

The other requests, written in my notes, identified jargon he would like to see and a schedule for our bi-weekly status meetings, which would be performed by phone, as the Colonel works internationally. I would be able to spend time with him on a single day or two every third week of the month. Too, there is a request for simple things to be included in and excluded from the writing. There was not too much of any particular request or restraint that I could not handle with ease or minimal scrutiny; I would be independent to handle the structure and form of the book as I pleased, and I am comfortable in knowing, in my direct belief, that he will be thoroughly pleased with the outcome.

I left the beautiful home euphoric with the reality that I now have work. It will grant me a less restricted life; it will enable me to purchase a phone to call people, and will allow me to take better care of my health and the physical ailments brought on by my poor surroundings.

I must conclude, dear book, in the midst of the moment-such glee-there is a sadness that has revealed itself, too. My expectations, and they were high, were to leave there today with a written contract and an advance to get started on the autobiography. However, the Colonel stated that he wanted to finalize his due diligence, and he wanted me to address the issues in the notes I had taken today; then we will meet again in two more weeks to make a final determination and agree upon a start date and cost factor. In a noble effort not to push him into a decision in which he was not ready to make, and imply an offensive ploy, I allowed the conclusion to be what it was. My observation is that military people of such high rank and authority, unless in the immediate battlefields and front lines, do not necessarily always make decisions with such haste. They are surrounded by the 'red tape' of Government and it swallows them whole at times; and so, they must have ample time to think and make decisions. It becomes habit in such people and is to be expected; I concur.

The exorbitant two-hour taxi ride in that rickety car consumed my last three nights salary from the store. While I hoped to get a nimble start on the notes at hand, it will have to wait until I can recuperate the funds in a few days.

20th of February, morning

I awakened early this morning and felt an urgency to write before I leave to meet with the Colonel; I feel that I need to compose something to soothe my nerves; often writing has a sedative effect on me; you know this too well, oh book. Next, it is important for me to survey myself before departing to the taxi station. I worked every day since our last dialogue and have saved enough taxi fare for the round trip or trips to come. Plus, today we should make a deal and I will return with ample revenue. I should like to impress upon you, dear book, that it is my intent.

The address? Check. The notes from our initial meeting? Check. Money for taxi? Check. Oh, listen to me; I am the one sounding like a savvy military man; perhaps the Colonel is already rubbing off on me. What a noticeable persuasion!

II.

20th of February, evening

Well, I do not know whether I should scream or throw myself into the river! Of all things to consider, the latter sounds more appealing! It seems a scornful reflection of my life-unpleasant to say the least!

While it certainly was evident, this morning, of my intent for the day's long journey with a successful result, it simply didn't end in such a way. The Colonel stood at the door restlessly waiting for me, as I was an hour late because the rattletrap taxi had a blowout along the way. And as I didn't allow him to drop me directly in front of the Colonel's home, for the sake of embarrassment, I managed to walk the final two miles to get there. If it is any consolation, though, the taxi driver agreed to cut the rate on the next trip. Whew! I am afraid that there may not be another trip if my decision to not return holds strong. Rats!

Why is it the world see's poorness through a prism? The Colonel knows of my desolate situation; that I am crushed by poverty; I opened up to him. He knows I am a man fraught with frugality and despotic means. But, to take such advantage of me in my despair is, in itself, frivolous! I am deeply offended by his offer of $6000 to pen an entire autobiography! This will take several months to complete. Has he not indulged in any thought on this issue? Such a prominent one! And even more so, a down payment of $1300? Whew! I spit at the thought of it! To make matters more hurtful, when I became taken aback by the offer, and he witnessed my sudden body motion and facial gesture, he raised his voice and gave me a demand, "If you are interested show up here first thing in the morning to commence interviewing me. Oh-nine-hundred- sharp!" He continued his snide words. "Take it or leave it." I stood there with a malignant irritability and blank face and suddenly I thought to be careful; any foolishness, in words or act, and I may betray myself. I left with a fake smile on my face, shook his hand, and thanked him for his time. I knew with certainty that if I returned, it would be in the morning at nine o'clock; bearing this in mind in the event I *would* take the offer. But I've not determined yet such thing, such senseless thing! I have an evening to contemplate such resolution.

Oh, who am I fooling? The more I have given it thought, the more this overwhelming sensation has gained mastery over me. How repulsive it is to treat another human in such a way! It completely abandons the benevolence that this world is intended to experience. It steals away passion and reason from a man in despair. It is cowardly & abject! I have become so malicious and mistrustful of my fellow man; some days there is an immeasurable repulsion for everyone and everything that surrounds me; today is one of those days! Arggg! Such treason!

It is late. I must rest; I know. Oh book, I cannot at the moment; I have a decision to make; it is a simple, yet practical one of such preponderance. The unvarnished truth of the matter is clear: the funds would allow me to find a better place and purchase the writing material I need. Perhaps I could visit the dentist and allow them to do only the x-ray procedure; that would start the process, at a minimum. It is a thought to admonish; just think, tomorrow I will have $1300. When was the last time I had such funds in-hand? At the end of the autobiography I will receive the balance. I could be frugal in my ways until then, this is true. Work can continue at the store but it would have to be days as my best longhand occurs in the evenings, long after the sun has fallen. Yes, I could make this work.

It is even later now, book, past two. I still cannot sleep; as much complicity remains from the day and I am obstinately mute; I pray I was not too ill mannered and discourteous with the Colonel. In reality, the situation doesn't look so bleak. And, as the case may be, I can tell, the Colonel is bearing financial issues as well. I recall when I had a home and vehicle and all those fanciful things of vanity; certainly, there were issues of economics associated with managing the whole of it. Well, it is almost undoubtful, then, that is the reason he must work and travel so far away; it assuredly is a matter of money. He must be a consumed and fatigued man from such onerous work and travel. Oh, I should be more grateful for the opportunity to provide such service to one; I should be beholden to him as he accepted me into his home with open arms. Too, he provided a grand conversation and a fine tea and French cake; such fanciful sustenance to offer a vagabond; an anemic and scrofulous little man like me. Oh, and the bag of dried figs-the ones with the long stem. Undoubtedly, they hail from Morocco; they seem of the type.

I shall see the Colonel tomorrow, or perhaps I should say in a few hours; and I shall do so with the utmost of pleasure and conviction. That is my decision.

The autobiography could only be written with an open soul; the greatest of all works are done with a clear head and a kind heart. I shall see the Colonel and, as God is my witness, shall endure whatever is necessary to bring about the tasks at hand. Oh, book, you always seem to give me the answers. You never elude me. I sleep now.

III.

21st of February

Dear book, dear fine book, my arms were filled moments ago; I could not have fit another commodity in them! I am so excited to have returned home in such a way that I am compelled to initiate our correspondence for the day. Oh, dear friend, I have so much to tell you!

About the things I have to store away-they are useful things that the beloved Colonel has given to me from the heart. I have a bag of pasta, the green type; and there is a large smoked ham in a can. Two large, beautiful lemons that I shall fill a plate with and place on the window sill-it will be the only thing of color in this place, hee hee-two complete and intact heads of broccoli, unmolested, three marvelous green and one beautiful brown pears-directly off the tree from his back yard; I picked them myself. And, of more importance, he provided me with enough pencils and papers to write three autobiographies! Oh, but the ham will have to be eaten quickly as there is no means of keeping it cold and the winter season is not here yet. I will just take enough for a couple of days and bring what remains to the family up the road a ways; that is what I will do.

But back to the day, my dear friend. Today was the first interview day. I was nervous enough at first but the nerves settled with the coffee; it was hot, bitter, and from Panama; I just knew it. In the first twenty minutes of our meeting I felt held hostage to lend an ear about the story of the cats; oh, how provocative. How kind and gracious the Colonel is to them; their treatment is first class, like children of sort.

Dear book, I am hyper and cannot step away from my giddiness and joy! I am perplexed by such splendid happenings in my life. It is a joyous time, a time for free-for-all and hullabaloo, if you will, ole boy! I must buy spirits to share with my stomach and my soul on this blessed day; this fat, dumb, and happy day. I will return to you shortly dear companion and tell you all about it.

IV.

23rd of February

My word! Time has passed quickly by; too short-lived in fact! My silliness and laughter, fraught with celebration, lasted longer than expected. The simple debauchery I anticipated with such delight became a mere two-day drunk!

Oh, the little devil standing on my shoulder tells me to be sad about this all. He whispers in my ear that I have challenged my own sobriety of many months; that I have 'fallen off the wagon'. But, little devil, it is a new day in time. I've precious opportunity in front of me; I will not squander such of my own future away as before. There have been many lessons cultivated from the dreaded ways and disappointment of the past. The future stands in front of me now; it is clear and virtuous and I shall manage it will ease and commitment.

My journey today will consist of the purchase of a phone and the necessary sustenance to make it through to the next visit to the Colonel in a fortnight. How candidly teasing and foolish the memory is! I just stored away several weeks' worth of food in this cabinet without doors!

09th of March

Today the Colonel broke his silence about some of his military missions; they were complex, well planned, and thorough. Though I propose not to rehash stories of blood and guts-that never makes for a good bio-it is the relevancy of his essential duties and responsibilities that, ultimately, make the story interesting; leading soldiers into battle on the frontline, capturing the enemy, performing interrogation on captured combatants.

Opening with a story of the preparatory basic military training, the Colonel told of how one of the most precious medals worn on his chest was earned from the grenade range, where he was given the meritable designation of Expert. In this story it wasn't a matter of how well he pulled the pin, aimed, and threw the grenade. No, it was a matter much more significant than that. You see, book, the run-down, drained basic trainees with the short, cropped hair stood one by one in a pit built of concrete mason blocks and a red dirt floor. Next to them stood an instructor, as they prepared to perform the duties of throwing a live hand grenade at a stationary target in an open field. (*"Arming the grenade, aiming, and reaching its intended target"*), as the nominal military nomenclature would have it.

Well, the young redheaded trainee standing next to private Modd was somewhat of a lackadaisical young man, always seeking attention, buffoonery, and comedy. He did not take direction well and pursued a nap in nearly all classes; for that he did loads of supplementary running and calisthenics. We shall call him Potts. As the instructor assisted Potts in the appropriate arming positions with the live grenade, as he had done countless times before, he gave the verbal instruction of "at my count of three, pull the pin and do nothing else beyond that." He started. "One-two-three." Potts, standing erect and with his body at an angle pulled the pin just as he was instructed. As he pulled it, the instructor stepped back a foot or two to allow the young soldier ample room that was needed. Through his intense nervousness and quivering, the young Potts turned to look back at the instructor as he stepped back, and while doing so, inadvertently dropped the small, galvanized steel grenade pin from his left hand. As the pin hit the red dirt, both he and the instructor stared at it. Through this immediate loss of concentration, coupled with intense nervousness, Potts dropped the live, armed grenade on the ground immediately in front of him. "Grenaaaaaaade!!!" A panicking instructor screamed as he clutched the young, soldier who was beginning to crouch to the ground in fear. Private Modd, being in the next pit to the right, watched the developments, as his own instructor had not yet made it to his pit. In the blink of an eye, the young Modd grabbed both Potts and the instructor by the shirt collars, and, in that same split second, rotated them all around into his pit, all falling to the ground. The explosion shook the entire area next to it and no one was injured.

Potts was reprimanded and, three weeks later, for some other imbecilic matter, was thrown out of the U.S. Army with a dishonorable discharge.

Hence, that is why his ribbon from the grenade range is Colonel Modd's most memorable. It is deserving of a man who possibly saved other's lives, even as a basic trainee.

Continuing on, Colonel Modd told the story of some of his Army Ranger Training-Hell Week as it is frequently called. During this week the trainees, which by this point have already received a position within the Army and have been hand-selected to attend such training, are parachuted into a large forest area and expected to survive for several days without food or water. Too, they must perform navigational duties like finding targets, obtaining information about "the enemy", who are highly experienced Special Forces soldiers hiding in this forest area, and evading capture. If they are captured, they are taken into a POW camp and interrogated. The training is extremely demanding and mentally and physically breaks many who weren't broke before in the recent weeks of the high-stress training; it is famous for having the highest washout rates in the military. This is the final test to becoming an elite soldier.

As the hours passed by and Modd trailed through the forest using his freshly acquired navigational skills, he became tired and irritated, and chose to get off the path and go down to the river he could see through the darkness of the trees; at the river he could drink water and take out the broken Snickers bar he had hidden well in his pants. While he was bent over cupping a handful of water someone suddenly rushed him and tackled him to the ground. It was one of the instructor soldiers. He immediately smacked Modd with the butt of the gun and "captured" him for the short, painful return to the POW camp, where eleven other young trainees had been captured, put in a room, and tied to chairs.

Each trainee was slapped and shoved around until it became uncomfortable, as part of the training. Their faces were placed deep into a large pail of water until the discomfort became immense. At a certain point several soldiers disclosed information exceeding the typical "name, rank, and social security number" that the standards of military indoctrination identify as the basis of information to provide an enemy in the event of capture; as a young soldier, you are taught this from day one. But, as the days passed by and the instructors ate and drank directly in front of the tied-up trainees, and as the beatings and imitation drowning's persisted, the young inexperienced soldiers began to drop like flies, one by one. The highly experienced Special Forces instructors untied some they felt were proficient throughout the training and had not succumb to the demands, and allowed them to leave. Most others, though, were simply told they were out; they had not made it.

The young Modd, now tied in a chair and exhausted from the drowning simulation, stayed strong and continued to tell himself that it would be over soon, even as the harassment continued. He remained aloof of the fact that there was only so far the instructors could go. But they, too, remained vigilant, and struck him and belittled him for even more hours, as he became the final soldier in the camp. Finally, they untied him and shoved him out of the door. After the four-mile walk through the woods, he reached his intended target and the training was declared over. Although he was the last one to make it, the young unsophisticated Ken Modd would win the prestigious "Best Soldier" award and place the even more prestigious Green Beret onto his head.

27th of April

The interviews every two weeks have been going as planned. I am obtaining a masterful insight of the Colonel's military and CIA time. The psychological and emotional aspects of being a military professional with such responsibility must weigh deeply on a man's resolve. The stress would tear an ordinary man down; break him down to the point of seizure and decay. Just listening to and recording such accounts is harrowing.

Colonel Modd surprised me today. After I concluded my final interview, and as I was placing my belongings back into the satchel, the gracious Colonel handed me a key. He told me it was the key to his home, and that he would pay me an extra twenty-five dollars a week to come and feed and clean the cats as well as pick up the mail. Oh, I am ecstatic and I feel honored that he has such credence in me; I cannot fathom that I have done anything to deserve such a distinction. I can use the additional funds for my means of sustenance, certainly. It is a blessing to be thought of so kindly by such a sympathetic person. Though I have not personally had animals for a long time, I feel confident that I will be able to take care of them as my own; this should not be a mind-boggling task.

18th of July

With each trip to the Colonel's home I am becoming more and more skilled in extracting information on the life of this great man; pictures, documents, videos, and other materials have become instruments in assisting me in knowing and understanding his life. The structure of the book is coming together well; much better than I initially perceived. It is becoming increasingly clear that the autobiography will indeed reach some level of success.

To get to know a human better, it is essential to have an understanding of one's surroundings. The photographs and videos tell remarkable stories; an author cannot feasibly and successfully create without such illustrations. To have only been in such places as Pakistan or Sudan, for instance, and to smell the atmosphere-to walk the streets-would have attributed so greatly to the success of my endeavor. My imagination, though striking, could never reach such a level, unmistakably so.

19th of July

After leaving the U.S. Army, Colonel Modd was recruited by the CIA in a pot cafe in Amsterdam. He was seated at a table smoking a joint and reading a Hemingway novel when a tall, blonde man with tiny blue eyes approached him. He told the Colonel virtually everything there was to know about Modd's short military career, his personal file, and even the people he surrounded himself with. Certainly Modd was irritated by it all, but stayed calm in light of the circumstances. To sum it up, nine weeks later he was completing training at the CIA headquarters and would soon be on a project.

Colonel Modd, now no longer a man of rank, but a civilian contractor, managed several programs for the CIA; they were typical, short-term, failed programs that needed some expertise to turn them around to meet new schedules and budgets. But, as straightforward as that sounds, they were in austere and hostile places like South Sudan, Uganda, Afghanistan, and Pakistan-not exactly paradise.

On one particular program, Modd was chosen to work with the State Department as a Program Manager, by way of the Central Intelligence Agency. The project site was Kabul, Afghanistan and the location was directly adjacent to the existing Embassy-defined once as the most dangerous place on the planet. The objective was to use an annexation of the land next to the Embassy to build a camp for incoming State Department and CIA brass. There was an extremely large amount of work to be done, including demolition of an existing Bakhazi stadium (the game with the goat heads being thrown into a small circle on each side of a field while the players advance on horses; essentially, soccer by horseback), the excavation of millions of cubic yards of existing mountain silt that had penetrated the valley over the course of decades; it was too soft to act as structural fill by any means, and the addition of new, hard dirt that could be compacted for the foundations. Then came design and construction of the camps to house the personnel.

As the project came into existence, Modd was introduced to his U.S. State Department counterpart Ed Cragley. Ed was a Foreign Service Officer on his last hitch; he had two years to go before retirement. So, as Project Manager, Modd reported all status to Cragley and, on limited occasion, Cragley would be driven by an armed caravan to the well-guarded site next door to perform a walk-through and assessment. Then he'd get back into his vehicle while being assisted by the heavily armed security team and wheel off into the sunset again, only to be heard from in emails for the next few months.

The project moved forward; the stadium was demolished, the unusable soil taken out, and now the entire nights were occupied with dump trucks coming in and out, bringing in the new fill dirt to be spread and compacted. The security, meanwhile, was very intense, with each truck entering and each truck exiting undergoing strict measures, including having security personnel walk-throughs with mirrors and bomb-sniffing dogs. And so, as it was, Modd worked in the evenings, with the understanding that that was the time for the highest chance of an incident to occur from the local militia groups expecting to make a name for themselves or competing with the Taliban movement.

Modd, an expert in languages, picked up the local Dari Afghan language and began to communicate on a colloquial level with the local Afghan guards. Be it known that, at the front of the property stood the security gate that everyone and everything had to pass through. Next to it, and with great importance, was the Afghan Defense Ministry, which was always guarded but more heavily guarded in the evening time. Modd began to befriend several of the local nationals that worked as guards on the property. His best friend was an old local man that cleaned his office each day; Modd brought him plate lunches from the local Turk restaurant and, after a few weeks, gained a trust in him that was quite strong. It is widely accepted in the Afghan culture that elderly men are greatly respected and, in this case was quite true. The younger men almost bowed down to the elder as he passed each day to enter the work trailer where Modd spent much of his time.

At one point in the project there was a skirmish amongst the local workers. The day shift superintendent had cut short the prayer times in an effort to get more work done. When this became known, Modd set a new precedence of allowing the Afghans to pray even more often. He suddenly became widely accepted into the community of three to four hundred workers. And so, his entrance into the gate in the evening time only required a smile and a firm handshake; rarely did he need to flash the yellow laminated ID card. Still, Modd continued to collect valuable intelligence on the workers, their families, and all of the contractors and vendors associated with the project. It was a plethora of valuable data for the CIA to use, especially considering the population that lived so close to the undesired U.S. Embassy.

Weeks passed by as this highly visible, highly important project took form. Each evening Modd would enter the gate at nine o'clock, hand off packages of Coca-Cola's to the head guards, then go off into his work trailer for several hours; it was typical of his routine. But one evening, as he arrived at the gate, the pattern had changed. The head guard for the Afghan Defense Ministry waited at the gate for Modd; the two had never met prior. Upon arrival, the guard introduced himself in rough English, and, as another guard translated, gave his many thanks to Modd for the

Coca-Cola's and other gifts in which Modd had returned from the states with (remote control cars, Victoria Secret magazines, and Levi's). The guard was ecstatic, but cautious, about meeting Modd that evening and this was the first of many meetings in which the two gentlemen would converse and share a friendship. On a number occasions, the guard, a Punjab from the northern states of Afghanistan, invited Modd into the highly coveted and protected Defense Ministry building that no one was ever allowed into, not even the local guards who watched over the project site; they were considered junior in rank nonetheless.

On the first occasion, as Modd recalled, he was blindfolded and forced to sit in a chair with his hands tied behind his back while everyone drank tea and spoke of associations between the two cultures. According to the guard, it was only for precautions, as he had never introduced an infidel into such sacred ground; his superiors would cut his hand off if they knew of such malaise. With each subsequent visit the precautions were slowly eased. Finally the two, and the guards' interior team, where able to actively hold conversations in the building with no threat expectations. Modd was even allowed to bring in his own sidearm.

On the very early morning of December 20th Ed Cragley, Modd's U.S. State Department counterpart, made a surprise visit to the front gate at the compound. Early in the morning, and unannounced, Cragley felt it safe to walk around the Embassy site to the newly annexed site to visit and examine the status of the ongoing project. He was, though, complicit in determining the threat that may or may have not existed, and broke protocol by doing so. And, without his knowledge, the threat existed and was a clear and present danger. The drugged-up guards from the Defense Ministry were tipped off that a very senior person had left the Embassy compound and was walking to the annex area. The highly coveted "Blue Badge" gave it away. As Cragley reached the front gate, ten minutes from leaving his office, the annex guards (local nationals hired for six dollars a day to defend the entrance to the project site) had already had their throats cut and were replaced by the Defense Ministry guards. These guards, however, where not the same guards in which Modd spent time with, but others who were only interested in the kidnapping-for-ransom of a U.S. Embassy official or high-ranking military officer. It was a scheme of the third shift guards that had been concocted and had been in the planning stages for quite some time. Now, it was in full effect. They arrested Cragley, blindfolded him, and quickly took him into the building, where they placed him in a dark room.

Modd lived away from the Embassy compound, at the DynCorp site in Green Meadows; it was a safe house area known to few local nationals. At four-thirty in the morning two men in suits & ties appeared at his door. After being told what happened, Modd was instructed to go to the Embassy to be briefed on the matter. Once there, after going through the security entrance protocol, Modd was rushed into a room, where he waited for an hour before someone came. The head of Intelligence for Embassy Kabul along with the local CIA Station Chief discussed the situation with Modd. They were interested to know how much he knew about the floor plan of the Defense Ministry building in which Ed Cragley, a senior Foreign Service Officer, was being held.

Modd knew everything about the building. From the previous meetings, he memorized everything that a human mind could feasibly recognize. From the amounts, sizes, and locations of air conditioning ducts to amounts, sizes, and locations of doors and windows, to the number of electrical sockets and telephone lines- he remembered it all. The CIA demanded he share such information. He did. He illustrated the floor plan of the building to the requestors as though he were an architect. And as a result, a team of commandos was put in place and rescued Cragley from his captors. Three Afghan's dead and a safe Foreign Service Officer. Modd received a medal of honor from the CIA for his work.

IV.

12th of August

It has not always been like this, oh book; this wretchedness, this squalor. I held a heavy workload at the University; not too heavy always, but gruesome only at times. I lectured twice a week; sometimes three times, and gave tests. My hyperactivity surrendered; the routine became stagnant after several years and I felt compelled to write novels.

One year, on the first day of the semester, while it poured down raining, I showed up drunk-early, but drunk. Nobody except me knew I was drunk in front of a new class of incoming freshmen. They listened with heightened anticipation of what lie ahead, took notes, and paid no attention to my stupor. I acted as well as I could, almost stumbling across the small trashcan, and my words were loud and rigid when I spoke. It was the only time I showed up fully punch-drunk and I gave much thought to the potential ramifications of such actions thereafter.

As the years passed by, so did my enthusiasm; the pay and benefits became more important than everything else and soon boredom challenged me more than the lesson plans and lectures. I had no superiors, except for the Dean, and he spent more time on vacation, using the days he had built up over a forty-seven year tenure. So, in essence, it became a redundant world where I simply "cut and paste" the previous years lesson plans and tests into the present years work schedule; I lectured less and less and depended more on the students to fulfill their own educational needs. Most certainly, though, there were always one or two exceptionally gifted students that demanded my time; they've gone off to be successful writers.

After a typical day at the University I slipped into my old blue Volvo and drove back the hour and a half home; within that open three hours a day I verbally recited most of the structure to be encompassed in the books; so it was a useful and valuable time. More and more, though, the writing weighed on me heavily. Soon I would be spending less time in my professional work and more time engulfed in research for the novels. When I was at the school, I found myself, as I sat at my desk in the lecture hall in front of sixty-two students, reviewing and editing work for one of the books I was about to ship to the publisher. I had come to my senses, though, and realized that my own mind could not successfully do both of these chores simultaneously and I began to awaken in the middle of the night to write. At least I could leave the writing at home and fully concentrate on my professorship and the needs of the students. I soon hired a young Arab to drive me, getting my sleep on both trips.

The first book "The Conditioning of a Man" was the hardest to develop; there were many times where a long span prevailed in between writings. It became challenging to the point where I almost gave up; neither the words, nor the storyline, came easy, and I put so much resistance to my thoughts. I tried to manage every single word and sentence; I tried hard to be proficient in every word structure. But I realized, at some point, that I was fighting a losing battle. I just needed to keep it easy and allow the words to flow. The whiskey helped. The pills helped.

After three years and three books, all of which successful, I set the pencils down and did not write again for four years. I do not recall the reason why my fervor and compulsion for writing had changed. This was the time that I started to experiment with heroin, so maybe the introduction of such new friend took me away from the passion I enjoyed and needed to complete my life.

As my second wife had died of an aneurysm and I lived entirely alone in the large red-brick two-story home, I began to use up the personal time and vacation days due to me from the University; I had not used of these benefits and was able to stay away from the campus for almost ten months at a time for three years. This was when I developed the most rewarding and acknowledged of all my books, "The Distance Between Fenceposts". Locked in a dark room, alone and quiet, the internal guide that I relied on so heavily for the thoughts lead me in a particular direction. I tried as best as I could to get my self out of the equation and allow the mind to put it all together. And so, it was a mind, filled with whiskey and heroin that assisted me in creating this masterpiece in which I won several awards for.

Barely eating, I lost weight. While consumed in it all, I overlooked the care that my own body needed and became sick on a few occasions. I thought to take up walking and each time I attempted to, as I was a mere half-mile down the road, I would turn back and rush to the writing, as something new and very important had entered my mind and needed to be included in the notes. I was beginning to forget things at this point, and I gave that little thought, too.

When I showed up in New York to get my award from the Writer's Guild, like all the others there, I was skinny like a broom and hopped up on booze and heroin. Oh book, it was a happy time of my life where I showcased my success. The folded up napkin in which I wrote my acceptance speech, which I still keep, reads, "It has been an excruciating struggle to reach this destination. At first, I stumbled, fell, and hurt myself. I got up. I stayed on the same path and I fell again. Once more, I got up and brushed it off. I stayed on that same path and continued to slip, even if only a little. I didn't fall, but I decided to take a different path. It was such path that got me here. Along this particular roadway there were signs that read, ALLOW and ACCEPT. I followed these signs."

When the concept of allowing the words to enter my mind, no matter what the prolific and scattered thinker wanted, and the other concept of accepting such words without resistance merged, telling the story became the journey itself; it became something I began to do with ease.

14th of August, morning

Though the bottle of whiskey went down well last night, I felt good when I woke up this morning. I've been anticipating all morning my trek to clean and feed the cats and put the bills on the counter; it is high time to get back to a labored way.

As the altered state of a humanoid who has been present for fifty-five years, I bear witness to the gap, which exists in everything. In music, there would be but a singular noise, where it not for a gap between the notes. In reading, everything would make no sense if a gap were not to be found in between the words. Sometimes at the exacting moment of a shift, a gap is found. It is where true intelligence lies.

There are shifts that occur irregularly in humans; big shifts that move their apparent life in another direction. Sometimes these shifts are so dramatic that they completely turn a life situation around. And, too, there are other shifts that bring calm and ease.

The humanoid Barron finds an item that will bring a shift into the life he calls his…

-Within Thought-

I.

14th of August, evening

   I must fully question my own self today, oh book, either through analysis or a failed memory! Could the drug addiction continue to exist, even though I am clean? Is it possible, or even plausible, that I continue to lose my memory? I am taken aback by my day at Colonel Modd's; to the point of sincerely questioning my own memory! I know that I write continually to preserve such memories, and perform the proper checks and balances, but, as the last few months have passed by so quickly, I am at a loss for events that occurred only recently; as recent as last week. What I must do-I am certain-is check my notes to validate my findings of this day.

   As I cleaned the cat's litter box today, I followed the trail of wetness-cat pee-into Colonel Modd's closet. While I bent down to clean the carpet, I observed a rather obscure book resting next to a pair of his house slippers. It was a large book, unquestionably consisting of seven or eight hundred or even nine hundred pages; it's binding made of simple, common brown paper.

There was neither a title on the front nor any writing on the rear or side tabs, so I could not determine precisely at that moment what it was. A thought came into mind that, as with the photos and videos, perhaps knowing what the Colonel was reading or studying would be helpful in my own undertaking of writing his autobiography. What a wise idea, I thought, so I picked it up.

Randomly, I put my index finger on a page on the right side, opening the book there. I began to read the cursive writing from the blue ink on the page. It was a handsome writing, orderly and clean, and could only have been executed by a perfectionist. What I read, at first, seemed somewhat obscure, perhaps contrary. Amazingly, it sounded like a similar story in which the Colonel had recently told me, but with major changes. I did not study it long, only scanned through it quickly, closed the book, and deliberated for a second.

I did not think for any length of time, as, again, I opened the book randomly to another page and viewed the writing there. As I read through the first paragraph and started the second, I recalled a similar story that the Colonel had shared with me in our interview two Friday's ago. I read two more pages until that chapter ended and another started; I stopped there and closed the book. Again, I closed my eyes and subscribed to a few moments of thought.

I stood there, perplexed, even confused for a few minutes; at least until my mind had a chance to come to order. Truly, I did not understand the events that were unfolding in front of me; confusion set it in and my heart raced.

I decided to take the book with me; which I've now identified as the Colonel's personal diary. "Lord please forgive me of my sins", I begged as I looked into the sky, for I am certainly not a thief. But, as my mind cleared, my sudden will was to go to my friend Semya and ask him to print a copy of it for me; I will work for the cost of the printing; do what is necessary to pay. Abruptly, I shall return the book to its location afterwards. Oh, dear book, my nerves were shaken; they still are. I fell that I will be stoned for this.

15th of August, morning

After he listened to my somber story, and with great intent in his heart, Semya opened his print shop for me and gave instructions on how to lock up when I finished; I worked in the evening time as no one were there. He said that I owed him nothing-that it was a gift-and he thanked me for the ham I delivered to his family earlier. Oh, I am so grateful for such kindness from this neighbor, one of God's children; it is never my intent to steal from my fellow man, nor to bring such harm. I worked there until four this morning printing a copy of Colonel Modd's diary; it was extensive work, but serious and necessary.

The taxi raced quickly to the Colonel's home so that I could replace the book; I was so nervous-fraught with the fear of getting caught; I sneaked the small whiskey bottle into my jacket. Rahman the taxi driver did not like me drinking alcohol in his car so I hid it and drank from only a small straw. Perhaps the interpretation of "stealing" was incorrect in this case and I was only creating problems for myself, I thought. The Colonel would not return for a month this time, so, really, there was no need for panic. Will I replace the book in its proper setting, just as I found it next to the house slippers? Was it on the left of the slippers, or right? What if the Colonel thinks that I rummaged through his belongings? Oh, my! I have set myself up for complete and utter failure! Why did I have to open another man's personal book? Of course, it looked like a special book, like a private book; I should have respected his privacy. I should have taken the time to think about it. Oh, I must call him and tell him the terrible news. No, I must tell him when he returns.

I found peace and calm for a few seconds, dear book. I made the time to commune with stillness. It will require some highly quiet and somber time, perhaps sitting in a tree. The other mind tells me perhaps to be in a tree is good, with a noose around my neck.

15th of August, evening

I returned the diary, and now I have my own copy, printed on stiff white paper with large columns on either side and a long empty space at the bottom so that I can take notes. Oh book-my quiet and impartial friend-my intuition tells me something is aloof here; my stomach turns and my mind races and I feel vehemently that something is not right.

II.

2nd of September

My beloved book, I have spent these last few days reading random stories from my copy of Colonel Kenneth James Modd's personal diary. I do not believe I have slept more than three or four hours in the past several days of study and have failed to eat. My eyes droop and my head aches but I cannot fall asleep.

I stand with insurmountable repulsion! It is with an empty heart and scalded spirit that I give you the bad news-the terrible news-oh book! My heart is as empty as an abandoned water well; my spirit is burned and scorched as badly as a wrinkled candle resting in an old drawer resting in a barn!

Friend, oh words of wisdom, I have been calloused in ways that exceed my imagination; in ways that I could never convey my esteemed literary talent to explain. For four decades I have represented my triumphs with morality and graciousness. I have had formidable success in placing empty, shallow words onto pages and aligning those words with others to create masterpieces. I have been handed awards of excellence of the highest accolades because of my literary intellect. The DNA in my blood stems from a generation of folk with the highest literary proficiency from around this world.

Today, dear book, I stand here speechless, wordless, and breathless. I will explain shortly after my return from a visit to an old friend. I need her now.

III.

9th of September, morning

Exactly a week has passed since I abandoned you, darling book, and I am deeply apologetic for it. The deep, fearful emotions that have sent me into a longing depression have made it feel as though much more time than a week has passed. I have been able to control the dysphoria with the needle; much time has passed since our last encounter.

The cold thin and white substance that seeped into my small veins from the sharp, thin stainless needle has been an invaluable source of solace. When the pinpoint edge breaks the first layer of skin and as it enters the second, it is a little painful. But as the liquid moves nonchalantly through the channels, it communicates directly with the mind and gives it relief. It is immediate relief that I am pacified with. Such injustice and ruin that I face is harsh and tormenting.

When the heroin wears off, the whiskey helps. I shall rest now, oh book, as I have much to tell you and I must be strong.

9th of September, evening

How despicable a human! Beyond doubt despicable! How could a man sit three feet from me, complacent, face-to-face, peering into my eyes, and tell me such lies? How could a man, without even blinking, without a cheek shivering or an increase in his heartbeat, tell me about his life in so many ways, and feel comfortable and gratified doing it, knowing all along-every moment-is such lie and deceit? Such falsehood?

Colonel? What Colonel? This man never has achieved such rank! His own words from his own diary, written by his own hands suggest that he didn't even make it to Sergeant. A Colonel? What a blatant lie! What deceit! The mere fact is that he got into trouble on two occasions and lost rank from each. He was a mere private! Oh, what a fool I have been to believe such fallacy and indignant untruth! Hell-forgive me, oh book, for my words-he is the fool that dropped the grenade, almost causing the deaths of others around him; he became drunk the night before and barely made it to roll call the next morning. His fellow trainees showered him and made him drink coffee. Lie! Lie! Lie!

Not many words of the story of Panama are true, either. Oh, to give him little credit, Modd did play a role in the invasion of Panama. He told me that he was a co-leader in a mission to capture the top eight military leaders close to General Manuel Noriega. In doing so, his team apprehended a valued asset that exclaimed to know the exact whereabouts of Noriega. Modd went on to say that the mission was abandoned, with the sole purpose of verifying the intelligence and arresting or killing Noriega.

The Special Forces team silently killed eight guards and made their way into the compound. They found Noriega sitting on a white leather couch, watching Gunsmoke, and drinking a Cubra Libre. With all guns pointed directly at him, Noriega asked, "What took you so long?"

I listened to this story with sincere gravity, as I vaguely recalled the television news and the reports at the time when this conflict was ongoing. My own family was visiting South America at the time and so I listened to the story with great interest. I read now, in Modd's own diary, the truth; that he was simply one of the hundreds that parachuted into the jungles of Panama weeks before. I find out too, that he became lost and disoriented but finally found his way to the highway that leads to the Bridge of America, near the canal. He stopped a passing vehicle and paid them twenty dollars to drive him to San Miguelito, which was in the green, safe zone. There, like a coward, he sought refuge amongst the thousands of civilians that remained, surrounded by heavily armed U.S. Marines.

This boldface sequel of lies, drafted into a slapdash story-one that I believed sincerely-is another testament of Modd's fraudulence.

10th of September

The tall tale about Afghanistan was not all true, either. In fact, as I duly express, the story was completely turned around and twisted for his own gain. I've read the same memoir in his diary and, though my memory may be failing me, I am certain it is not the same account I heard this putrid liar talk about, as he stared me in the eyes in the comfort of his own home, amidst the roving animals.

The diary says, yes, Modd was a contractor for the CIA, and yes, he was working at the embassy in Kabul. But there are many contradictions from the original story; I shall endeavor to explain, dear book. When Modd arrived at the front gate of the compound where the project was located, it wasn't Coca-Cola's or Levi's he distributed from a brown paper bag to the local guards from the Afghan Defense Ministry. No, it was bottles of whiskey that he had procured from the embassy exchange. And yes, while Modd went into the Defense Ministry building on many occasions, joining the Afghan guards, he did not go (as his own words state) to socialize or speak about business. He went for the purposes of smoking hashish and drinking of the freshly opened bottles of Johnnie Walker Black. Of course, all the while, learning the ins-and-outs of the building; its footprint, floor space, and mechanical and electrical systems.

So, as previously mentioned, Modd was not doing honorable deeds, but merely drinking and using drugs with the militia groups that would inevitably kidnap Ed Cragley, the State Department Foreign Service Officer. It is true that early in the morning Mr. Cragley attempted to enter the site to perform a visit, and it is true that three guards from the Defense Ministry kidnapped him and brought him inside the building. And certainly, without heed, it is true that they were asking for several hundreds of thousands of dollars in ransom, knowing that they had a captured a key target for their militia leaders.

My anger lies herein, though, specifically, with the remainder of the story. Early in the morning agents knocked on Modd's door as he lay asleep. They escorted him through Kabul to the Embassy for questioning. With certainty, they knew that he had gone into the Ministry building with the guards on several occasions, and that he had exchanged whiskey purchased from the embassy Annex, and that, openly, he smoked hashish next to the guard shack on numerous occasions, day and night. With twenty-four hour, seven-day-a-week surveillance on the building, nothing was overlooked. The spooks lying in the prone position atop the Embassy, watching through high-powered night vision optics saw everything coming and going-every movement was noted; nothing was missed.

Several senior-level personnel held conversations with Modd in the early morning hours on this unnerving day. He told them that he memorized the floor plan of the building; that he knew every single thing about its systems; every nook and cranny. At first, he seemed quite eager to help, but then, at some point, he just shut down, not giving up any much-needed information. Frustrated that he was possibly circumventing them, the Embassy leadership team left Modd alone. He sat in his chair giving no responses; leading them astray as a cat walking in a circle.

After several hours of silence, a Marine one-star General walked into the room and introduced himself. As he dove into his speech and started discussing the significance of time in kidnappings of such high value, Modd interrupted him and stood up, obviously not wanting to hear any of it. "Sir, with all due respect, I would like to have the CIA station chief for Afghanistan here to speak with me." The General responded to the request, which he would make happen. He shook Modd's hands, and abruptly left the room. Though several others attempted to pacify him, Modd stayed closemouthed each time, discouraging each of them. Some threatened physical action and some, legal action; Modd invited it.

At three-forty in the afternoon, a tall, thin, and wiry white-haired man appeared in the room and identified himself as the Station Chief for the CIA in Afghanistan. After, he stammered, "What is the purpose of all this nonsense Modd?" He asked as he walked forward to the desk, approaching Modd in a non-threatening manner. "Why don't you just give us the floor plan so that we can go in and extract this hostage? Don't you value this man's life?" He remained silent for a few minutes and patiently waited for Modd to speak. He didn't. The Station Chief continued, "I know what it is you want. I will give you $30,000 in a briefcase, cash money-US dollars-no questions asked." Modd looked at him candidly, blinked, swallowed softly, and replied. "I don't want money. I want a hard copy of an Engineering degree and an MBA from my local University. I want a full set of legitimate University transcripts; just as though I attended without missing a day. That's my request sir." He concluded. The tall white-haired man stood in awe as he yelled, "How in the hell am I supposed to make such a preposterous thing happen man?" Quickly, and without hesitation Modd interjected. "You made it happen for David Marcellus." Stunned, the Station Chief hammered, "That is top-secret information! Where did you find out about this?" Modd reciprocated. "I know you can do it, as your predecessor did it before, when you were his deputy. You sat at the same table as the negotiations were being put together." Knowing he was broken down, the man then asked. "How much time do we have?" Modd replied. "Less than forty-eight hours." He continued, "Oh, and sir-one more thing-when you formalize this, I want two witnesses in the room and a paper trail, so we have no complications." The tall, thin, and wiry white-haired man raced out of the room defeated. Modd knew how cunning the CIA could be-as equally as he-and made sure that there would be a full agreement, and others equally beholden to it.

As we see, my good book, one in which I have inscribed in and trusted for years, I am dealing with a man who values his own life ahead of anyone else's, a man who is willing to risk others' lives for his own greed. How staggering and even hideous of a soul! Oh, he has no soul-to knowingly defy a government agency where people risk their lives to protect our citizens?

I am sick to my stomach with it. My insides turn as though I have eaten a horse; I prayed that this would all come to a fair conclusion, that this would be the beginning of new beginnings for me, that this new course I would set on would set me free from the poorness and despicable surroundings I live in. What a scornful reflection on my life; I have been wronged. I should put a bullet in his head. Were it not only to make my own wretched surroundings even worse (life in a prison), to live in a smaller, more cramped habitat, to have to eat foul food-when I do eat-to have no access to drugs or booze, well, why would I do that to myself? Oh, but my God has not listened to me; he has not heard any of my prayers. For I believe in him that he is master of all, and I believe this is not the path that he wanted me on; not a path of complete and abject failure; crushed by poverty's existence!

I will seek revenge in ways that's make you wish your heart did not beat Colonel Modd. Whew! What disgust I say the word 'Colonel' with! You don't even deserve to have a name; you should be nameless! My vengeance will be so forceful so as to make you mental and seek an asylum; there you can tell all the lies to everyone and they will believe you; they will fall prey to your indulgence, narcissism, and aggrandizement. My vengeance will make you bow down before yourself and pray and beg for forgiveness of all of the lies and immoral ways. You are revolting. You are despicable!

13ᵗʰ of September

My indulgence for the last three days has been very substantial. As my madness has rendered me incapable of reasoning, of caring for myself, I have once again tasted the methamphetamine; it was powerful and stinging on my lips and gave me chills. But in a fleeting way, it took away the pain and the grief that has been handed to me from you Mr. Modd, and it makes me more powerful. It shifted the illness of thought away until I felt nothing.

Oh, my dear book, my old friend and soul mate, I feel that I have forsaken you in so many ways. I speak unkindly of another soul, I feel hatred for a man, and I seek vengeance. It is not my usual way. For if not the drugs to calm me and the whiskey to ease these pangs, I know not what other choice exists; I am devoted to the escape and gratification of the alcohol and drugs; they compliment my hunger and my thirst.

In the last few days there has been much apprehension, sitting on the floor in this corner with my back resting on the wood slats of the wall. The pool of urine that remains underneath me is a warning. I have either reached an end or am at a fork in the road and must decide which way to go. I am not sure there are any other options.

IV.

11th of November

I have been too tangled in the practical matters of conceptualizing a blueprint for my revenge of this decrepit mole of a man, oh book; it rips me to shreds to be away from you for such period of time. There is only a hundred and thirty-seven dollars that remains in my pocket. It is all I have, and I will use every ounce of it in conceiving, planning, and executing my vengeance.

In a couple of days I will catch a bus to Chicago to meet with Underground Publishing Company. They have reviewed the manuscript and requested my presence.

12th of November

I reached Mr. Petrovich, the Vice-President and Editor-in-Chief of the publishing firm. We held a lengthy conversation about the manuscript. Recalling the conversation, I feel as though I were a little shy. But I must be diligent and vehement is painting the picture I have for this new book to be successful. I cannot allow myself to be some weakling with crouched eyes and a whimsical handshake. I must be compelling! My dear book, here is the plan:

I will create an entirely new book. In doing so, I will continue to meet with the despicable "Colonel" at his home and I will make it seem as though it is business as usual. From the interviews, I will get him to discuss all the stories possible, and then I will make comparisons of them with the memoirs from his own diary. The end result will be a new version of the chronicles of Ken Modd's life. It will expose the lies and delineate the truths.

I think it to be a remarkable idea, and as I expressed to Mr. Petrovich, addressing me as professor, it will be my finest work to date.

Mr. Modd will have no suspicion of the goings-on in my mind, he will only become conscious of it at the very end, when I hand him a copy of what he thinks is his autobiography. It will be more painful that a bullet in the head and will ravage him mentally for the rest of his life. It is a brilliant and remarkable saga to this queer and complicated journey. My vengeful ways will be assertive and admonishing!

13th of November, morning

I am now sitting on a bench and feeding pigeons in downtown Chicago, nervously awaiting my appointment with Underground Publishing. There is not much else to think of; such engrossment has been done. I will embark on this new quest and my retaliation will bring success. The birds are hungry, dear book, as I.

13th of November, evening

Ah, the wonder of it all! The discussions went remarkably well. I thought it would be just he and I, but surely, I had to explain the undertaking-oh, not the vengeance itself, but the writing endeavor-to a gaggle of about twelve people. I sold it in such a way as only a man who finds a teaspoonful of gold in his backyard, and now has a conviction to dig up all of the yard, would.

I acquainted this team with the new manuscript with ferocious animosity, terror, and dread. I did not blink for an hour as my cheeks were flush and my heart rate screamed. Early in the conversation I stood up, clenched my fist, and pounded the table. I am certain my eyes gleamed with malice. I made it very clear of my intentions to write the most earth-shaking story a human would read; all the while, in the silent and restrained background of my mind, keeping my attention on the planned revenge to the other storyteller.

After I shared the short nine-page manuscript of the new book, and gave my intense vision of what it will be, the publication team left the room and I spent a few more minutes speaking with Mr. Petrovich. I had shaved, put on the new coat, and shared a bottle of whiskey with a stranger as he shined my shoes last night. I did not come into these offices looking like a vagabond; I gave no idea to anyone of my poorness, my wretchedness-my true-life situation. In fact, I will have to recite fifteen Hail Mary's for the lie that I told; that my limousine driver had driven me from afar and was waiting on me downstairs. I feel so despondent that I have told such an untruth to another person, especially one that is trying to assist me. I am sorry, oh book, for diving deeply into the waters of untruth, as I hold such conviction to make this only exceedingly rare behavior.

Mr. Petrovich asked me to be seated in the foyer area, next to the elevators. I waited for him about twenty minutes and he came out with a paper in his hand. He said, rather loudly as though I were deaf, "I know you already have a hotel, but I feel terrible that you have had to make your own arrangements; it is normally something we take care of when we bring a potential client to our offices." The paper was remittance for my next two nights at the Ritz Carlton on 6th Avenue, where I led him to believe I stayed. As I turned to walk away, Mr. Petrovich stopped me and asked me to wait just two more minutes; that he had one more thing. Calmly, but with frenzy inside, I did. Soon, he walked out of the twin glass doors and handed me a check. "This is for the gas for that beautiful limousine." He said. "I have never seen a brown limo before and that one, well it's just fine. I shall see you tomorrow." I simply nodded and said thank you. Every cell in my body wanted to counter and say, "Oh, I'm sorry that is not mine", but I imagine at that very second that my mind fought with each one and warned them to stand down. Whatever happened there, on a psychological level, turned out to be best and I shall not allow it to eat me up inside with guilt.

14th of November

I did not drink last night in fear that I would compromise my early appointment today. I was able to cash the $700 check at the hotel last night, ate a good meal, and slept well. Now I am filled with an unfound level of energy, one that I haven't experienced in quite some time. I anticipate the final meeting with Mr. Petrovich today with hope, promise, and goodwill towards something unimaginable. And though I am experiencing a new level of vigor, I cannot escape from the fact that revenge, one of life's most powerful poisons, eludes me.

15th of November

I am on a Greyhound bus now headed back to the ragged shack. I have much time to write and share my experiences with you, dear book, as the reality of this all begins to trickle in.

Yesterday Mr. Petrovich invited me again into the conference room. Once more, I thought we would be together alone, but that was not the case. The owner of the company, I must have forgotten his name and did not leave a shallow impression by taking notes, was invited to the meeting. The others that sat in the previous discussions were there. "Professor Desulfer," Mr. Petrovich started, "It is routine, here at Underground Publishing, for our personnel to sit at the table and give a final greeting to writers who may have potential opportunities with our organization." After each person gave a single general thought about the project, they proceeded out of the room. I stood up, shook their hands, and extended kind words as each departed; it happened quickly.

All who remained in the room where Mr. Petrovich and myself. He began to tell me about the risks that publishers take and the statistics of successes and failures. He stated that, of every hundred manuscripts that come across his desk, and his company sees 600 to 700 each month, that only less than five percent even have the opportunity of moving to the next review. As he rambled on, discussing statistics and risk, my mind uncharacteristically drifted off to negative rationalizing. I just knew that what I had to offer was not something that they would be interested in, despite my experience and previous success; and I had completely wasted my time; that perhaps I should have given this more thought.

I only spent a few minutes engaged in the negative thoughts and, calmly, as I realized the uninteresting subject of statistics was over, I refocused. "Professor Desulfer, last night everyone you saw in this room, including the CEO of this company, sat at this very table until almost one in the morning. Compiled of over 300 years of experience in book publishing and editing, and with success with some of the world's greatest writers, our team has never seen anything quite like the subject of your manuscript. It is alarming, yet powerful! The conception and ideas are created almost as if it were truly happening. We feel this will be a commanding and immensely profound work of art once you complete it kind sir."

My disordered and jaundiced mind waited guardedly for the heartbreaking "*but*" to be added to the sentence. He continued, without hesitation. "Professor, it is with great regard that I offer you, that Underground Publishing offers you, the sum of $230,000 for a finished book. Of that, you will receive an eight percent advance to get started." He continued speaking of trivial but practical matters involved in the contractual agreement, but my mind remained somewhere in the previous statements and paid no attention.

When he finished talking, I remained tight-lipped and motionless, not exhibiting any indication of concurrence or rejection to his offer. Other than just to sit still, remain calm, and look at him, I did not know what to do. My conflicting mind began to quickly question if this was real, and for a second I did not know if I was asleep, filled with alcohol and drugs, and was having a dream, or whether it was true and I should strike myself to prove it.

So, for several seconds I waited it out. To Mr. Petrovich it looked as though I was formulating an analysis of his offer, that perhaps I was calculating the math in my head. The absoluteness of it all was that I was in shock. I stood up, unsmiling, bent forward with eyes wide open, and stared at him from above. I watched his eyes droop, his smile depress, and his shoulders fall, as he sensed I was about to reject his offer. I allowed it to happen, simply to watch him; I am certain I took pleasure in it; I took it all the way until the end. I told him that I needed to make a call, but really didn't; it was for show. After the perceived phone call, I came back into the office and told him it was a handsome offer and I accepted.

We exchanged paperwork. The transaction generated for him my signature on twelve pages and for me a check for $18,200. I felt deeply lamented by the trade, as though I had more than I deserved-like I had taken something that wasn't mine.

When something new such as a condition or event occurs in a humanoid, at the immediate onset of this new experience, there is a singular affair that occurs in the very second of its existence. This, I have made notice of in the humanoid population. It is the exact moment in which an idea is formed from the energy of thought. It is the absolute basis that forms decisions of the humankind mind.

From the very second in which Barron clearly understood the impact of the event which drove him to a paralleled anger, his madness-his unconsciousness-has grown. It has capitulated into an internal rage in which he seeks revenge at any cost. It is this second, this spark, this abrupt brightness of light that propels humanoids forward. This very energy guides them to greatness; business leaders, engineers, artists, writers, and so forth. To the contrary, and with misery to illustrate, it is this very energy-this organic stimuli-that sends a humanoid to the very prisons that he constructs.

There is a path that Barron must choose.

I.

6th of December, morning

Well I cannot, for the life of me, explain how, when, or where I have come to be constrained in this hospital bed for twenty-one straight days! The wires and hoses that are attached to me are piercing and causing a labored discomfort while I lay in a single position, unable to turn.

The nurse read the chart to me without looking up at me; she seemed more embarrassed than I did. It stated that I had an overdose in the strip club at eight in the morning and an ambulance was called for me. She said it was a mixture of methamphetamine, cocaine, heroin, and prescription painkillers. I am not sure these doctors have made a sound analysis of my laboratory findings; that is my hypothesis. I did nothing more than cocaine and alcohol. These medical facilities and there fanciful quacks thrive on ceding false diagnoses for the purpose of meeting profit margins! And I am appalled by it!

I do recall some of the chivalry and celebration on the night that I returned from Chicago. It was a momentous string of events that occurred and, while I wait for the nurse to come and take this excruciating IV out of my arm, I shall infringe on my memory so that I may share it with you, dear book.

When I got off of the bus, I walked down to the business district and began my day of socializing at Tim's bar on 52nd; it could not have been any later than two. I do not recall what time I left there. I do remember where I went afterwards. Fool heartedly, and without haste, like a man on a mission, I walked into the gentlemen's club-Hearts. Per se, while I was not seeking love, nor answers, oh book, indeed, I was seeking companionship and communication.

I stayed seated for a couple of hours in a corner and watched the events unfold, as drink upon drink were served to me; they were really weak drinks so I ordered two at a time. The dancing ladies passed by my table and I lowered my face to my drink, hiding it momentarily and pretending only to be disinterested. As they passed by the table, noticing my inattention to them, I raised my head again to take another view from a different angle. After several drinks and some time, my racing mind calmed, and in that stillness, I came to the realization that I had over $18,000 in my pocket. I pondered on it for several minutes before a woman of Asian descent sat down at the table with me. She invited herself and her friend to my table and we held a well-mannered but simple conversation. I asked if they would like some cocaine and they said yes and I told them that I had just run out, hoping they would be able to supply me with some. And they did. They asked if I would like private time with them, the two of them together, and I gave the green light. It had been a long time, a very long time, since I had endured such beautiful conversation with such beautiful people. It was arranged that the room would be ours for the next few hours.

The drinks continued to flow in and the translucent crystal tables served as a drop-off point for the thin, finely cut lines of cocaine. My sexual journey with the Asian women was no longer a mere fantasy but a provocative and sensual occasion-and a costly venture for an impotent man.

I did not pay attention to the time, nor did I care. I was engulfed in celebration and, periodically, reflected on my purpose for rejoicing; I thought about my vengeance and how it had become an endearing and purposeful part of my spirit; how it would embrace my soul with joy and burn the bridge of sadness that now exists. But, I must add with severance, such thoughts only lasted temporarily as the outside world in which I played became more real as the time passed that evening. I have no recollection of anything else; I recall bright colors and a hologram of a girl dancing alone in a wrought iron cage. That is all.

6th of December, evening

I have reached home now and I am vibrant to have returned; I slept much on the bus and have regained the energy that I need. I will not be so toilsome to myself about the unintentional overdose, nor will I belittle myself for having too much to drink, for it was a stellar occasion that was necessary. It is a major victory and I celebrated with all my heart and with all of my energy; I will not succumb to the zealots that try to explain away what is good or what is bad; what is right or what is wrong. If I have done something intentional to put myself in such a position that I would overdose, well then, I am sorry to no one other than me; and no way was it something done deliberately with intent to cause conflict.

I seek retribution to a man that has harmed me in significant ways, and I have celebrated my successes in formulating the ultimate plan to rid him of his narcissistic and self-serving behavior, and too, I will never divulge to him, until it is over, what my intentions are, and while I look at him directly in his eyes, and listen to his falsities, and pretend to write them and pen them as a true, proud, and eloquent professional would, I will laugh inside at the insidiousness of this all and be thankful to my God, the only one I know and understand, that I had this opportunity to seek an eye for an eye-to impair him, to abuse him, and to break him; for his name is Ken Modd, dear book, if it is even that. Yes, that could be false, too.

II.

9th of December

I sat there on the white leather couch today staring at the same art on the wall and in the hall and on the floor. They were the same pieces, all in their respective places, at the "Colonels" home. But today they were not as lovely as I recall them several months ago. They just reminded me of dust.

He wondered why, oh book, I had not been back in almost two months. I did not lie; he would not have the pleasure of a lie from me, as he is below it. I told him I was sick for a while and I was in serious contemplation about what to concentrate on next in my writings. I said the truth.

Modd asked no more questions, but I trembled inside as I sat there, looking him in the eyes, with deep-seeded thought, and writing notes-penning his lies. This day he would depart from the truth again and tell stories of how his "work" took him away from his family, and he lost two wives and children. I am not deep enough in the reading of the diary to have come across words about his previous marriages, but I fathom this story, one supposed of love, to also be a fable.

Though I sat on the white couch in the same writing position, with a mobile desk in front of me and a lead pencil in my hand, I did all in my power to keep myself composed and be who I normally am when I am in his home amassing notes for his autobiography. But I could not help but wonder, as I looked further into his eyes, not even glancing down to write, as is my custom, whether he felt me as I felt him. Could he tell that things were different, things had changed? Then I thought, if Modd were the man I truly write about in this autobiography then I would believe-no, I would absolutely know-that he possesses the wisdom, experience, and the energy to feel my revenge; but this man, this imposter, probably could not feel the concept of energy that exists in anything. He is cold and calculating. He is motionless and greedy, and manipulative at heart. I die to know where such hatred for mankind has come from. It is deep within and must haunt him terribly.

I continued to think, oh book, that he, oh the great Colonel Kenneth James Modd, must have grown up with a silver spoon in his mouth. Forgive me, oh friend, for judging another. I cannot shy away from what I have read and ultimately learned about this scoundrel. I believe I have the right, that I am warranted and I conceive gravely that, in exchange for the displeasure-the enormous pain this man has caused me-I am promised with the right to judge him; I shall not be embedded with guilt.

Modd must have come from a rich home. He must have got his way every time he whimpered. He probably had a weekly allowance that was more than I make at the family grocery store where I sweep and mop.

Oh book, he has a big surprise coming; he has earned it. As I was closing the tablet with the notes that I took, I felt his hand on my shoulder. I closely witnessed the confidence he exhibited in me and I returned a smile and said thank you. And I said thank you while smiling on the inside, too. It was, on the outer surface a pleasurable smile, not too much; not so much as to raise the cheeks, or allow the eyes to squint, but a simple smile to keep the energy level not negative, but not positive; just a neutral smile with nothing else to add.

And when I got into the taxi and along my way, that smile did grow, oh book. It did grow. It was a calculating smile.

III.

3rd of January

The partying has left my soul, and the celebrations gone with it; it is now time to intensify my focus on the venture at hand; time to advance. I am a true professional, I am a novelist, I am a professor at wit, and I will create the most monumental novel that the world has seen! It is my aim!

The first decision I have made, oh book, is to stop chasing random stories in Modd's diary, close it up completely, compose myself on the couch with a glass of whiskey and a vial of heroin, and start from the beginning of the narcissistic fool's diary.

4th of January

Mr. Petrovich sent a text today to remind me that I had eleven days remaining to the first milestone, titling the book. It has already been done. I have given this considerable thought, and as several options have come to mind, there has only been but a single fit. I believe I have the perfect title for the new book; it is pure and exact.

The book, as I endeavor to explain, my dear journal of self, is about a man who has had immeasurable struggles with honesty and forthrightness. It is about a man whose own inner trials, whatever they may be, have restricted his life, controlled him, and made him the tyrant he is today. This conflict-this waging of war-is the chasm that lies between a man's own terrible lies and deceit and his own truth; written by he, himself. I shall title the book "An Alter-Ego Speaks."

18th of January

Mr. Petrovich called today, oh book. I did not expect it. The hangover weighed heavily on me early morning and I could not hear the phone. But I reached him later. He requested the first progress report of "An Alter-Ego Speaks." It is a cumbersome and useless spreadsheet that burdens me too much. I am tired and will do it later.

Be it not for you, beloved book, I would not have known this action were necessary today, but I will continue giving you my words of thought and provocation. A total of 22,208 words have been written to-date. Only half has been through a first edit, and the manuscript has been fine-tuned to give me a perfect synopsis of the book.

I have to admit that, so far, it has been much like playing a game. I am matching his truths with his lies, almost one for one; and though I have not delved yet into his childhood or juvenile experiences, I am of the belief that a similar pattern will emerge in his youth-the scoundrel. Here is an excerpt of his words:

"The fine-edged, shiny blade rested against my throat and I could feel its sharpness slide warily over each hair follicle as it methodically coursed further and further down toward my Adams Apple. My heartbeat exceeded two hundred pulses a minute and my blood pumped rapidly against the inner surface of my skin, so rapidly in fact, out of the corner of my eye I could see my heart beating from the veins in my foot. The cold steel chair provided no solace as a sharp pain climbed up my legs, over my buttocks, and rested in the upper lumbar region of my back. I looked deep into the Iraqi mans half-shut green eyes and read nothing. His quite disposition, even as he placed firm pressure on the freshly sharpened nickel blade, made me more nervous as time crept forward. I said nothing; all I could do was observe his restful, callused hands move sluggishly, without a tremble or quiver. My mind raced, my heart thrust, and my thoughts propelled as all I could think of was my family, and what my loss would mean to them and my friends on the boat fishing without me and whether they were thinking of me and whether those thoughts were good thoughts or simply thoughts people have after funerals when all the cake has been served and the wine drank and the tears spent and the conversation now is only about stopping at the Wal-Mart to get coffee filters and diapers and I wonder if the subject of me will resurface again maybe in a day or maybe a week or not until the first anniversary of my death. The keen-edged blade continued to scrape my throat and I waited for the short, plump Iraqi man to ask a question, to probe into my work, to get answers from me. He didn't talk;

he expected me to say the first word, to spill my guts. I didn't. As I pulled my thoughts together and took several deep breaths, unaware of what would happen next, he quickly yanked the sheet off of me and asked me to step off of the barber chair, as he had completed my haircut and shave."

(Ken's diary, pg. 389)

-Above Thought-

I.

2nd of February, morning

I have returned from sweeping the floors at the grocery store; it is such hard and consuming work; often I do not feel the need for such derangement. I am back to this shack where the only thing that seems to surround me are spider webs and brown dust. It is so funny, and makes me hysterical at times, but at this moment, I cannot even distinguish between what is a spider web and what is dust. Oh, what a scoundrel I must be to live so indisposed, hee hee! It smells of musk and the only color in the place comes from the lemons on a plate resting on the windowsill near the broken window.

The case of whiskey still fits well in the small closet on the porch, although the manufacturers now attempt to fool us with their smaller plastic bottles. I've booby-trapped the casing of the door opening in case the rodents want to make peace with my drink. That, per say, is something I should not forget, otherwise the next inhabitant would find an old man buried under cases of his own whiskey; what a miserable death that would be, I say!

2nd of February, evening

What I wished to do in this quite, cool but not cold evening, dear book, was to spread myself out like a butterfly, lay back on this couch that takes up so much of the floor space of this rickety shack, and write words on your precious white sheets. Because I was a little hyper at such moment, there were other things I wanted to do at the same time; my mind was racing and I could not choose.

The option I chose, to start reading Modd's diary from the very beginning, has me completely dismayed and breathless; what I read aloud almost made me choke on the pent-up saliva swaying around in my mouth. To understand it better, because I do not comprehend it by just reading it, I have chosen to copy each word directly onto your pages. By writing it down-the words of Modd's own diary-I can examine it and it can be a method of dialogue between you and I, dear book. It starts...

"I remembered it so well. She shoved her huge, white-skinned fat knee against my small head as I knelt on my knees with my face pressed in the corner. My small head was jammed in between the knee that was pushed forward with all of her body weight-all three hundred pounds-and one of the three brass hinges that supported the small closet door. Once she backed off a little, my body slipped downward to the floor, following the contour of the corner in front of me; the hollow impression formed in my head left from the brass hinge remained there four or five minutes until returning to its original state. She then stomped on my head with her large shoeless feet, and as I covered the head with my six-year-old hands and arms, giving it some protection, she worked on the body downward to the stomach, where she stomped the big fat feet and rapidly kicked there. Almost completely out of energy from quickly raising and lowering the huge tree trunk like legs, she now bent down and began striking my small head with her closed fists; on the large fingers were large rings with large square purple gems; each strike leaving its own indention. Realizing that her breath would be gone any minute and she would be left tired and wore out, she reached down and pulled me up to my knees by a handful of the hair on my head." Now stay on those knees you little piece of shit!" She screamed and screamed. Though the screams were as loud as a train, they provided some relief to me, as they were not nearly as painful as the fist and foot strikes. Too, I recognized (at such a young age) that she couldn't scream and strike at the same time for some odd reason. It was such an odd recognition. Struggling to catch my breath from the wheezing that normally accommodates heavy crying, and shoving my forearm into my eyes to catch the falling tears, I winced as the feeling of pain now began to labor and sift through this six-year-old body. I then shifted my motions from wailing into a slight series of soft breaths. At the same time, almost instantaneous, I turned my attention from the immediate and agonizing pain of the blows to a less drastic but constant, seething pain that could be activated by merely giving it mental attention. I studied my skin as the struck areas changed color-from a light pink to a purple and then black. I touched the area softly to not yield further pain. I looked forward into the corner that I knelt in, and concentrated my eyes on the missing paint area just below my nose. It was at that point I realized the mark, that of missing paint, was from my nose where it had pressed against the wall months before. I knew, as I grew, there would be more marks, missing paint marks appearing to creep up the wall slowly."

Oh book, for these words were so heavy, and I am fraught with fear! I could not do anything other than write them! I looked at them, and tried to read them in a way that I could understand, but they made no sense together! Individually, one by one, they seemed as common English words written by a young child with little education. When I placed them in sync, though, and I began to have a basic comprehension of the sentences as the adjectives, nouns, and adverbs flowed together, any perceived clarity turned into fog. For it was not a fog from anything nameless or remote; it was a premeditated fog in which my own mind created as a barrier to intentionally sever interpreting what lay in front of me on page one of Modd's diary. Confusion has laid its backlash on me, oh book!

There are no applicable words to describe my thoughts at the present moment. I am sitting here trying *not* to think, trying with all of my soul not to think; but on brief occasions, and in short intervals, thoughts pass through a portal and enter my mind; I am unable to avoid it. Although I am a man who has written books, published scholarly work, and achieved greatness in literary means, both as a human and a professional, at this moment I am at a great loss for words, much less a sequence to put them in.

II.

09 February

I thought it would be a promising idea to stop and wait a few days for my soul to heal before reading further in Modd's diary. I did not go anyplace except to the liquor store and my dealer down the street, my heroin connection (Note: Jimmy B. @ 3212 Portland Street, on the step, Friday mornings-7:2 0); it was a few days of rest that I needed; I desperately had to restore myself from the recent emotional turmoil that bewildered me and made me weak.

As I fumbled through the papers that lay sprawled on my desk, I picked up some of the pages from Modd's diary that I had been analyzing and glanced at them. A silly thought came about and when I first gave it attention it seemed quite foolish. Some twenty minutes later it reappeared in my mind; the same silly thought. "Would I be able to gain some insight as to Modd's current life situation, his work, his love life, his personal life by reading the last entry or two in his diary?" I could not get away from such a bizarre notion, but as my mind gave it more and more thought, it began to make sense.

The words, as most of have been lately, were so compelling that I felt the urgency to write them again, one by one. The very last page of Modd's diary reads as such...

"After I wiped off the last of the shaving cream from my face, and with the water trickling down my chin, my own eyes met directly with the ones in the mirror. I felt suddenly that time stopped. I stared into my own eyes and saw a clarity that I'd not seen before; and I understood plainly what it meant. As the stare between the two diminished and thinking reentered the equation, my eyes focused on the face in the mirror, giving attention to the scars on it. Attached to those scars, I know, are deep, painful memories. While the thin layers of fat under my chin could use some plastic surgery and Botox injections to help the wrinkles on the side of my eyes, those things seem minuscule in comparison to the significance of the scars.

Above my right eye, just above the brow, is a short scar left over from an incident forty-three years ago as a young boy. I said something to my Uncle that I wasn't supposed to say and the next time he wasn't around Aunt Mildred reminded me of it. As I stood there thinking about something that seven-year olds think about, she caught me blindsided with a backhand. The big purple stone on the ring that has left so many other scars in so many other places on my body split my eye and the blood hit the floor before I did. With that, I was reminded what I had said to my uncle and that it was something I should not have told him. It was a painful reminder.

As I smile firmly while looking in this mirror, I can't help but stare at one of the large front teeth with its left side chipped off. The dentist has repaired it on numerous occasions but it continues to break off when I eat a fruit or piece of meat. Each time I see the tooth I think back to the importance of telling the truth.

I lied to her, and lying to Aunt Mildred was something that should not happen. When I left school that afternoon, the little redheaded boy that had been bullying me all school year long waited for me in a culvert pipe next to the road on the path that I took to walk home. Unlike the rest of the days when I was too fast for him to catch me, this particular day he did. He punched me in the face a couple of times and I crouched down to protect myself. He kicked me once and as he went to kick me a second time he slipped and fell into the puddle of water on the opposite side of the culvert pipe. It had given me just enough time to grab my bag and run in the opposite direction. And so, I had to take an alternative route back home, and it took me an extra twenty to thirty minutes. As I arrived close to home, even a quarter mile down the road, I could see Aunt Mildred in her large figure standing in the front yard near the road with her hands on her hips, looking like a statue. As I got closer I could hear her loud voice screaming at me to hurry up, and as I got even closer, I could see the end of the belt, with the steel buckle, shaking back and forth in her hand. As I arrived in the driveway, she swung the belt at me haphazardly and missed, almost falling down. She swung a second time and I ducked out of the way and ran into the house, passing the neighborhood kids that were standing against the fence watching and frightened themselves. She cornered me in the house and asked me where I had been.

Instead of telling her the truth-that another kid had beat me up and caused me to be late-I told her that the teacher let us out late. She knew better because she had already called the school. She struck me several times with the belt and then wrapped the leather belt around her fist tightly so that only the metal buckle could be used. She punched me a few times with the buckle until I fell on the floor on my knees. Then she grabbed me by the hair and held me straight up in a vertical line. As I stood there crying and shaking she became still. Neither of us moved for a minute; we just stood there looking at each other. I said, "I'm sorry" and before I could get another word out she backhanded me in the mouth with an open hand. It was the same purple gem on the same gold ring that caused other scars on my young body.

Today I tried to use the hand mirror to assist me in finding the scar on the top of my head, but it was physically impossible. Funny how one can remember an incident from so many years ago. As a ten-month old baby lay in his crib screaming and crying from hunger and thirst, and probably a wet diaper, she lay in the next room getting laid by some guy who she had shacked up with before. This was the same guy that jerry-rigged the wooden second-hand crib that was supposed to have protected me as a baby. As I must have interrupted their playtime she barged out of her room screaming and hollering at me while running towards me. Whatever words and statements came at me at that moment, I am certain, were not those of love. She picked me up quickly and abruptly, held me high in the air and shook me, while screaming until she was red in the face. Then she threw me into the corner of the crib where the long screw stuck out. The bed sheets were filled with blood;

blood was on the wall and blood was on the floor. I remember this clearly, even as a baby. Even now I see it in dreams.

I wonder often why I am timid to look into the mirror and see a kind, handsome face with a few scars. But I do not see a kind, handsome face when I look in the mirror; such wholesomeness is hidden in the back layers of my vision, hiding behind the horrible stories. I see a face with scars and those scars are a direct, undisguised link to a stolen childhood."

III.

10th of February

For the life of me, oh book, I cannot explain why violence exists. I am not certain there are enough white, blank pages in this world to fill with ink describing its true meaning or even its origin. I am saddened deeply by my own behavior and even more so by the callous words I have studied from Ken Modd's diary. I have questioned my own intent and cannot find an answer as to why my interest remains. Like my own personal journal, too, I have found more than stories of life's conditioning. There is political satire, humor, and plans still yet to be formulated within the chapters of Modd's diary. He writes....

"There is an old song, "*I still haven't found what I'm looking for.*" At this point in my life I can apply it directly to my own inability to sit still and stay put. I looked up the word 'accomplishment' in the dictionary today. From its definition, three particular words stood out: fulfillment, creditably, and achievement.

I've sat on the rugs with the mullahs; more than often they were the bad guys. They control the people and they control the drugs; I don't care what anyone says politically.

I've sat across a table and held firm and honest conversations with a Sudanese General who had only recently come out of the bush. He had scar on top of scar; more scars than me. And I watched the challenges many of those Sudanese men dealt with, having to use a public bathroom for the first time. Most had never. There, I stepped over dead and dying people, animals, and plants. The noises they made and the smells they had still haunt me to this day.

I've swum in the Nile, Mississippi, Volga, and Tigris rivers. After I swam in the Tigris I saw many floating bodies-more than I felt like counting.

I drove through the steep and creepy mountains of Afghanistan and Pakistan, and I smoked hashish with the locals.

I made love to a prince's wife in Saudi; she begged me to take her with me. I collected intelligence from her brother while pretending to love her.

I've been on the receiving end of an IED and missed suicide bombers by five minutes-three times. Lost an eardrum.

I lived in a Russian dacha, in the middle of a beautiful forest; I smelled the wheat fields and felt the cold, deep lakes.

I walked daily from the Embassy in Kabul to the Turk restaurant down the alleyway, next to the main road. The best thing about that little trek was the beautiful little girl with the emerald green eyes begging me for a quarter each day. The baklava and lentils were spectacular. But the picture of me on the wall, offering a bounty for my head-the glue still wet-was my waning to say goodbye to the war-ravaged lands of Afghanistan. I am sure it was a message.

Two Chinese women in Dubai cost me a lot of money. What I got in return was priceless.

Seeing the Panama Canal from the air as well as under the water were remarkable experiences.

I've handed suitcases, plastic bags, and wet cardboard boxes filled with fifty-dollar bills to strangers; foreigners I did not know and would never see again; both of us in disguise.

I spent three weeks of my own time sleeping on the sidewalks of New York City after 9/11; volunteering at the Ground Zero site; segregating pieces of concrete.

Truly, my life has been a series of ups and downs. And maybe that's why I don't feel secure; all photographic memories of life as it has been have lost their luster. Living a double life, in so many ways that I can't explain thoroughly, even to myself, has not allowed truth and honesty to be integral to the way I am supposed to live. I have jeopardized the personal relationships I've been in, loving one thing and ignoring the other; there has been little balance for a long time.

What good are the accomplishments when you get old? Are they only now memories? Is that why there is not as much energy in the thought of the accomplishments as when the actual accomplishment occurred? So then, based on this theory, it is safe to say that memories have less positive energy in them than accomplishment does?"

IV.

11th of February

Oh book, in many of my lectures there is a single question that was asked almost every semester by the young, fragile minds of the freshmen. "Why does man lie?" And by all means, the young minds often made frugal attempts at answering such question. 'To save himself from a crime', 'To get a better job', or 'To make himself feel better; raise his ego.' It can be argued that there is no real answer.

Now that I've been afforded the opportunity to have read the majority of Modd's personal diary, of course without his knowledge, I have but my own theory of why this man lied all of his life and I will dictate such theory into a dissertation for the upcoming class.

Mentally, I glued together the falsities (from the notes I had taken for the purposes of introducing to the autobiography) with the true words written by his two very hands in his personal diary. My conclusion-my analysis-in simplicity, points to his life conditioning, entirely.

The lecture will conjoin with the violence in this mans life. It will highlight the overwhelming importance of the indoctrination of a young person as he gains insight into life. My intention is clearly to accentuate the very conditioning that served as the slave *and* the master to Modd. My memory is leaving me; today I am not sure what remains of it. I do not want to leave this world not having done this. The lecture commences...

LECTURE 01 VERSION 01

When a boy is beaten as a young child and he sheds blood, and that blood splatters onto the wall, and that wall becomes his prison-one that he kneels in and rests his nose in its corner-and he stares at that blood and begins to relate to what he learned of the molecules and atoms in the science class, that such blood was he. And he looks in the mirror and sees physical detriment in places that take his handsomeness away; and he learns, as he ages, that those detriments, those cuts and bruises and scars all have lives of their own; some staying for a short time-a mere visit-others a lifetime. He knows the scars will always be there, even when he, too, becomes an old man. He knows this because he asked old men about their own personal scars. He learned and he listened.

Ken Modd was beaten as a tiny, inexperienced boy. The beatings, though deadly at times, served as a maestro to him. As each incident occurred, with no reason but for a young boy being a boy, there was extensive teaching ongoing. He began learning early, with the pain of each blow, each strike. Then, as he grew, he no longer counted each hit on his body one by one, but simply counted the incident as a single beating; it seemed easier to deal with; one beating versus forty-two blows and nineteen kicks.

The grief, anger, and futile act of it all-the beatings-took their toll on the beater, too. Ken looked up and saw the red-faced, out-of-air Aunt Mildred gasping to catch the next breathe and admonish the next blow. He'd gotten so used to it that he knew the first hit after her gasp for oxygen would not hurt as much; she had to build her strength up before the strikes started to sting. The blood, the blows, and the agony of Aunt Mildred catching what would someday be her last breathe, became a strange tale in his mind, and the young boy thought about it often.

The physical abuse that Modd suffered his entire childhood was a precursor to a future of inability to lead only a single life in a manner conducive to what is labeled as ordinary, versus a double-life where untruths and unpredictability are the norm.

Ken "the Colonel" lied because fear existed in him. Certainly to live a life in which he lived, to work and reside in war-torn lands and see death and strife and be humbled by it so deeply, he was indeed a strong man; but a strong man with much fear deep inside. He trained in the art of war, not attaining honors, but just being there, in training, learning as little as he needed to to get by, barely making it through. But he was there, and he learned how to fight; I give him that! Yet, he always walked away or hid around a corner when an actual fight broke out, whether at a bar or in war. He wasn't scared of the fight itself; he was scared of his own anger, and what it would do to harm another.

Ken lies because lying as a child drew serious consequences, and that has reversed itself-a rebellion, if you will-and his independence at 15 years old insisted that he was now a man and he could do what he wished. When he remembers the beatings as an adult because he told an untruth (as a small, decent boy) there suddenly becomes clarity in his mind that the act of telling a lie was something no longer deserving of a beating or humiliation, but, instead, a choice. When he came to the realization that telling another person something untrue would never get him a beating again, not only did it become a choice that he could easily make by thinking or analyzing, but it became a gift he learned to relish in to his advantage.

There is a time frame in which a young child develops an ego. It is the "me" stage where every toy in the house, every pot that makes noise, and every good, funny colorful thing belongs to "me". His own childhood was not stable enough, for long enough, for Ken to develop such ego. He lived in constant fear, and when it is fear that controls a mind, it is an emotion that dominates fully. Hence, when he left home at fourteen, the first gift that was given to him, the gift of freedom, was something he knew nothing of.

He developed the ego quite suddenly as the days passed and he began to realize that the gifts of comfort and ease would come to him. And, though these emotions where not as powerful as fear, they still provided a level of comfort that he was not used to. As he got more comfortable it was easier to analyze his life, to determine what he wanted, and what he didn't want. But trusting something comfortable was not easy.

He made friends easily, but after a while-after the stories and grandiosity became too much-and his newly found ego stood out and took over, those friends disappeared; they were much further ahead in life than he.

Beginning young, making money, and having his own car, Ken was able to make friends easily. He told lies to have friends. And when they left, he told more lies to get more friends. It was a cycle of instability happening over time and uneasily noticeable.

He told lies to get into college; to get into the military. He told lies to sneak into the Baptismal room at his church so that he could falsify his own baptismal papers to get into the Army.

The partnership of lying and fear has existed throughout the life of the roving Ken Modd. He lied to his teachers in fear of getting a bad grade; in fear of the bad grade being seen on the report card; in fear of the beating and verbal abuse that would accompany it for the next six weeks until the next report card and the next bad grade.

He lied to his wives because he feared the loss of his independence. A woman stole his childhood independence from him and it had some merit. Marrying at a young age, without much experience in relationships, he was not allowed the chance to fully understand the vital importance of telling the truth to another person, especially in light of the rebellion to another woman-his Aunt. Too, he felt that the squabble and nagging of a wife (her need to communicate) who denied him some level of independence, even a trip to the bar for a beer, were ropes around his neck. He truly had no purpose at the bar, and would have really preferred to be home, but deep inside the burning of ego forced him.

As a candidate, Mood lied to prospective employers. As a jobseeker, he did not tell untrue statements to a prospective employer because he believed in, and planned, a career path and that career path was part of it all. He did not lie to an HR Manager to make himself feel better or feed a happy ego. No, it was the fear of instability that existed.He was scared to be out of work so long that he would be without money and the option of moving back in with Aunt Mildred may some day be the only one; he fears this in symbolic ways. He dreads it. Even the sanctity of marriage is not enough to fight such fear.

Point blank, Modd had no friends growing up; it wasn't allowed. There was a single convenience of having a boy next door of the same age. The convenience was that Aunt Mildred could send him there to play with the boy while she was romping with some stranger in the bedroom. After an hour, though, the yells and screams carried across the neighborhood, and it was time to return home.

From the corner of the fence in the corner of the backyard, Ken watched three different families go on their weekend outings to the beach, fill the driveways with cars with kids and with gifts for the birthday parties, and families loving and laughing together. He watched. When he became independent of that corner fence in the back yard, with a car and money, Ken made friends easily. He pumped himself up to the teenagers; they all thought that he came from wealth, that he was well educated, rich, and a young man of stability. Little did they truly know or understand about Ken.

And so, those lies to his young friends were not the only. His inability to hold a conversation fraught with truth exacerbated with age.
End of L1V1.

12th of February

I woke up from the couch from my afternoon nap groggy. There were no crazy dreams or arthritic joints giving me problems today; just didn't rest well. I sat across the small wobbly table from a book; I didn't even recognize it; not it's form, not it's color, or the words of its title.

The tears hung around the bottom edges of my eyes, not brazen enough to fall. I cannot believe-a book I have written in for over three decades-I do not even remember it.

That is the sad part, oh book; and there always is a sad part. But there is a looming dichotomy with everything in life; I remembered you easily, when I opened the cover and began to read the words.

The other apperception of mine today was that I had a face-to-face with the one who steals memories. Silly, though, I recognized it, too, for the first occasion in such time. It scares me to know that one day when my memory fades out like it just has, I may drift deep enough in memory loss to never again recapture your words, dear book.

When I began writing "The Distance Between Fenceposts", I was engulfed with work, a second wife, and the alcoholism that was just beginning to come to light. And so, my life was cluttered. I seemed to be going somewhere in my career, but very slowly.

Someone pointed out to me that I should become more organized. And so, I did.

I threw away seven different wire-bound notebooks, filled with six years of essays, critical writing, notes, comments, and the like; copied half, and threw the other half away, really. I began to think how I would organize my notes and the things that I write, simply because I wanted to rid the clutter of my life. An idea in a bookstore seemed perfect; a massive journal with hardback, nylon-bound covers, able to be used and abused from the hardships of opening and closing, with dirty hands often, the stress on the paper from the pen pressed too hard from a moments anger, and the ebb and flow of being the center of attention.

Everything I wrote went into that journal. Oh, I am silly drunk!! This journal in front of me, and yourself, dear book. Political stories, religious thoughts, opportunities and threats, too. There were personal love letters to and from, daily training notes, a contact list, and, within the last decade, as my memory has diminished, a daily journal.

Storing you in the dresser drawer worked fine the first or second year after the diagnosis. But, as it got worse, I noticed, the dates between writings progressively became longer and I was writing less often. But now, great friend, I keep you on the back of the toilet.

Every political speech given by Fidel Castro is in this book. The writings that excited me most, watching a certain ballerina dance for sixteen years, and complimenting her, live in this book. Life as it be in other places fills a bulk of it.

14th of February

My life is being consumed in the world of Ken Modd.
I've not left this rickety shack and this couch for so
many days now and I scour through his diary to find
purpose for it all. I am addicted to not only the liquid
and solid substances that these plastic whiskey bottles
and glass syringes fill my body with, but to the deep
superficial reality of a man's conditioning. My own
childhood, as I remember, seems a direct opposite of
his, containing none of the vile and ignominy that
engrossed his life. The lecture continues...

Lecture 01.22 Version 02

The words of Modd's diary illustrate a broad
division between he and his wives. My deduction
is that he was completely overtaken by the pain of
his conditioning.

As a kind and gentle man, on the surface, Modd
easily gave his heart to his relationships, doing all
he understood to keep them functioning. But,
through the years, the pain of his childhood
showed up often, as an uninvited guest. At first he
controlled it in a way that it only seemed a
singular event or cause, but inevitably such guest,
such monster, would rear its head more often. It

would be the trigger; the pain cells that lie
dormant inside would disrupt the calm events of a
day and cause irritation and an invisible hostility
in him. It would be that long-held subatomic
prisoner inside of him that would scour any reason
to find food, and the food was the pain that a
young boy had to live with for a childhood.

It is plausible that this man I have studied for
many months now lived the vast majority of his
life in a state of conditioning that outdistanced his
decisions and left unnatural circumstances and
disastrous results behind.

When this intense pain-corpse, this conditioned
molecular state he derived as a child, would
appear in his adulthood, intimidation would be
one of its many byproducts. He would smash and
break simple household items and use gestures
and evil looks to make his wife afraid; he would
destroy both her property and his own. On the way
to the bedroom he would take the pistol from the
drawer and wave it freely as though it were a flag.
He would kick or shove the family dog out of the
way and yell at it simply for sitting on his chair or
being in his way.

As Aunt Mildred aged, the less the beatings took
place. But it was too late to take back the serious
implications of the physical abuse that surrounded
him; the verbal threats were equally as guilty. The
intimidation stayed around; not much physical
strength was needed to illicit a stare that held so

much barbarous meaning; not much strength was needed to throw Ken's wooden sailfish that rested on the nightstand across the room and splinter into many pieces. And not much strength was needed to pull Uncle's belt down from its hook, wrap it tightly around a fist, and flash the worn silver buckle in a threatening manner.

This single area of conditioning administered to the undeveloped lad had devastating effects on his future relationships with women. The solution to it would have been to use non-threatening behavior in his marriages. The simple, yet completely unknown, vindication for Modd would have been to allow the woman to talk and act as if she feels safer and comfortable in expressing herself and doing the things she wanted to do. And, without doubt, such a vindication by Aunt Mildred could have potentially shifted many of the effects of Modd's own life and relationships.

The volume of emotional abuse handed out to the young adolescent was enormous, stemming from four years old (or younger) until a young teenager. To wake up in the morning and go through a day when another person puts you down constantly and makes you feel bad about yourself and your accomplishments must have been damageable in so many ways; living in a world where you are constantly called names and being humiliated has to decrease longevity of a human's life. To be made to feel guilty and to have some belief that you are crazy has to have taken its toll on the mind.

Too, to wake up next to the person that you stood at the alter with and, together, made a conscious decision to live together for all days, only to distribute such a level of emotional abuse as was given to you, certainly cannot keep a marriage intact. Staying in such a relationship would only bring harm to future generations; putting this pain corpse to rest-developing an understanding of this conditioning-is this only solution.

The answer here is to have the ability to listen to her in a nonjudgmental way, being emotionally affirming and understanding, and valuing her opinions.

End of L1.22 V02.

V.

22nd of March

It has been a while since our last correspondence, book. I do not remember much of what I have done in this time, nor did I remember what the last notes where. Now that I look back onto your soiled pages, I see where I dropped off a month ago.

Though the place still reeks of urine, I was able to find a razor in the trash pile outside to shave the long beard down some. It was raining moments ago and wisely I showered in it; I am not certain when the next rain will be. There are remnants of zucchini on the counter and two open bottles of whiskey at the foot of the couch, near the lamp. The lemons on a plate are rotted, but still yellow. They are the only things that give the place color.

Though, I am almost completely isolated from the world in these final and unnecessary days of my life, trapped in this bridge tender shack. There are spider webs and brown dust encasing everything; distinguishing one from the other has been abstract. What has not been missing, though, is my emotional attachment to the book that lay in front of me-this handwritten diary of a man named Ken Modd. I have a slight recollection of other responsibilities that are necessary, but it is important to keep the focus on this singular issue at heart.

Lecture 03.21 Version 01

This Aunt of his controlled everything the young boy did; who he attempted to befriend, whom he spoke with, what he read, where he went and so forth. His involvement in outside activities was monitored like a German spy. And through it all, there was jealousy to justify these actions. And as my previous lecture has been about his relationships, too, these relationships were aggravated by such isolation. There should have been trust and guidance; had there been, Modd would have been able to support his wives goals and respect her right to have feelings and friends. Too, he would have been supportive of her activities and opinions.

As a person who was most probably abused herself, chances are, Aunt Mildred was acclimated to the cycle of abuse. There is some evidence to shed here that her parents and grandparents where abusive to her. And so when one lives a life of abuse, it is easy to minimize, deny, and blame others for such castigation. When with a crowd and an acquaintance pointed out such abusive ways to her, Aunt Mildred would make light of the abuse and not take such concern seriously; it would also be a recrimination to that person attempting to help.

With such long-standing periods of abuse came the absolute denial of it; but the bruises and scars told of another story. Too, there would be the shifting of blame for the abusive behavior; pointing the finger at the young child and saying he caused it.

We can see this pattern of exploitation clearly in Modd's relationships. There should have been honesty and accountability. In both cases, they should have accepted responsibility for self and acknowledged past use of violence. They should have admitted to being wrong, instead of swaying from it. And, of course, the communication lines should have been open and truthful.

I cannot imagine what went through the mind of a twelve year old boy as he stood at the cash register waiting to check out and the only grocery on the conveyor belt was a box of tampons. From an early age, to be forced to clean toilets, areas high above the shelves where no one else could reach, and other ridiculous tasks that a hired hand should have been doing, if not the 'lady of the house', is confounding to the mind.

Using privilege was another extreme tactic of abuse the violent Aunt held in her repertoire. She treated Ken like a servant, forcing him to clean and do things (as a very young boy) that he did not want to-without even a minuscule allowance.

Acting like the 'master of the castle', she defined the roles of the home as it easily applied to her. Missing from that, though, was the ability for the young Modd to be included in decisions. The application of male privilege in his marriages, taken from years of conditioning, would serve in a detrimental sense for Modd. To make it work, there should have been a shared responsibility in the home. There should have been mutual agreement on a fair distribution of the work tasks and chores and the family decisions should have been made together, as a cohesive unit.

Right under the eyes of his Uncle, Aunt Mildred stole money directly from him as his work pants hung from the corner in the bathroom and his wallet rested in its back pocket. She stole money, while he gave her money, to fund her gambling habits. Sitting amongst eight or nine others, usually three to four days a week, she participated in local card games at acquaintances homes; sometimes sitting for fourteen to sixteen straight hours; only getting up to use the bathroom.

She had no work skills and rarely held a job, as the kind Uncle funded her life and lifestyle. She even made the Uncle ask for money when he had to pay for his own work expenses and ran low. When Ken obtained his first employment at the burger restaurant, she forced him to pay her half of his check to "help with bills." And, with that said, it was rare that she shared details of the family savings book with them; there was privacy that the family was told to respect, meaning "eyes off".

This behavior, this form of economic abuse-this conditioning-had an effect on Ken's marriages as well. While not marrying highly educated women seeking their own career paths, he was able to bask in the glory of using such abuse to control others, preventing them from working and having their independence. There should have been an economic partnership of sort. The decisions of finance should have been performed together and the benefit from any financial arrangements should have been mutual.

Through a means to get attention, when the card games where not ongoing, no boyfriends where around, and life seemed to be dragging by, Aunt Mildred drank to the point of disillusion with life. She became so disillusioned that she attempted suicide on a number of occasions. She didn't want to die; she just wanted attention.

End of L3.21V01.

25th of March

Modd writes....

"I took the yellow envelope from one hand and shook the other. Walking back to the private plane, I felt the envelope to see if it had something in it. I didn't see the need to open it in front of the 'suit-and-tie' that met with me; he didn't know what it was all about anyhow.

The stewardess served a cocktail as the pilot gave his verbal instructions. I sat there, high from the weed, in a daze looking out of the window, staring at the wings of the plane and paying attention to nothing in particular.

As the plane reached its intended altitude and I was served the second drink, I cocked the seat back and opened the envelope. I took out the two laminated sheets and stared at them. The first, a Bachelor of Mechanical Engineering degree, was embossed with the school emblem and dated and signed by the dean. I stared it down with intensity and thought briefly of what was to come. I glanced at the other, the Masters Degree, and put both back into the plain yellow envelope and closed it. There were other papers in the envelope but I chose not to go through it.

As I meditated, I thought about the events that lead up to this day. It has been a tough journey these last few years, flying in and out of these razed and decimated lands, driving patched-up vehicles through crowds of people who would kill me in a second if they knew it was I, an American man, driving past to get to the next checkpoint and beyond. They would take my eyes out, one by one, if they knew it was I collecting vital intelligence on their loved ones to give to my own government. Certainly, as I look back, it has been astonishing. But why would anyone risk life and limb in such arduous and challenging surroundings? I do not love the Afghans, per say. Nor the Iraqi's. Yes, they are mankind and I must love my fellow man, I must embrace him; that is what my own conscious tells me to do. I don't question the importance of such ambiguity, only my own sanity.

Am I sane to have come here, for many years now, and leave my children behind for the sake of money? It is only I who can answer such question. I sit here with two fake college degrees; handed to me by a representative of an organization that, by its own decree, stands firm for the other side of truth itself; in fact, its very essence is driven by untruth. I could not have made the money I have made here, in a tax-free situation, back in the states; and though I have tried to reach such level of financial pinnacle, it has been impossible. It would be impossible; I would have to work eight to ten years to make what I make here in a single one.

I can't, and won't succumb to the guilt that shadows such behavior. When I left home I did so for reason beyond what the normal young teenager would understand. And though there has been no definite, formulated career path, the goal was simple the entire time-do what is necessary! And I did what was necessary to send money back to the states to take care of the children; to give them what they need.

While I walked the dirty and dusty streets of Kabul wearing a woman's Burka and pretending to be a deaf mute while standing next to one of the most prominent war lord's clothing store and taking photographs of every single person entering and exiting, including children, it never crossed my mind that I shouldn't be there. It never crossed my mind that I did not have the education, the very education that "supposedly" is necessary for these high-paying jobs, or the skill to do this. To collect data and information to hand over to the CIA for analysis seemingly came easy for me; there were funny times, too.

What I cannot do, simply by admitting defeat, is fall into a trap where the guilt kicks in. I look at these false documents, and like the doctored Baptismal papers that I forged in order to get in to the Army Officer program, they appear real. Young men and women go through many years of hard work to get these pieces of paper. I chose not. First of all, I did not have the understanding of it all at that age; I was running. I was running from the torture and the sadistic ways of a family in which I trusted. That very trust was lost permanently when I walked out of that shotgun house. But when I left, life did not get easier, it certainly didn't. I simply walked into another world of torture and brutality; it was the world itself. My childhood was so foggy, so brutally contempt at keeping me blind from the elements of the outside world, that I was unaware of what was waiting for me. But like these people, these Afghans, I too would have given anything to leave.

There will be a day that I will have to tell the truth to my children about my education and my life. There will be no remorse. I did what I had to do. I sat in that building with those illiterate, passionless tyrants as we shared opium through the same wooden pipe and drank from the same glass of Johnnie Walker. And I understood the words of Dari when two of the eight told the others that I should be the one in which they kidnapped and sought ransom for; I pretended not to, but I did understand. They pulled straws.

And it was me who lay on the ground hiding from the bullets and screaming behind a garbage bin while I bled from a burst eardrum at the Serena hotel where the IED went off in the vehicle in front of me. And it was me who sat in the stopped Land Rover wrenching my hands on the steering wheel, as they sweat, while I stared all the way down the barrel of the Kalashnikov the very young and very black Sudanese boy held at two o'clock in the morning; he slowly reached into my shirt pocket to get the ten dollar bill; it's all he wanted.

It was me who stepped over that body and, not stepping wide enough, inadvertently kicked the bloated stomach and watched in dismay as it exploded and the blood and guts and liquids and even the maggots that ate them splattered me from head to toe; it was I who sat on the edge of my bed that night and cried about it all, all the while still smelling that smell and wondering over the course of the next few days, as I rode with my team members, if I still smelled of such odor.

It was I who found the hand at the ground zero site while segregating the large concrete pieces from the medium ones from the small ones. The hair on the hand and the Masonic ring served as a telltale sign that it belonged to a man. My only confusion, for many minutes, was *who* to give it to.

These events where all driven by my own choices. Of course I was not levelheaded in making most of them, as I was driven by survival. How can I live in a poor industrial state where the average income is less than $30,000 and expect to provide for my children; to make sure they have food and basic sustenance of life? How could I ever have enough money saved to give them a real education-not one like my own? When I made such choices, the only thing I had in mind was the future. And the risk factors where rarely considered, if ever. Had they been, I would have chickened-out so easily; I understand now why I never gauged the risk, intentionally didn't think about it. But I think of it now, and, for the love of my children, would do it all again if necessary for them to endure.

Certainly, they will know such information one day, but I am not so eager to talk about it now. And if they love me as I love them, they will understand it clearly, without remorse."

26th of March

   Though I cannot attest to what it takes or even what it means to be a father on a personal level, having taught thousands of students, I have learned to listen and discover many things on parenting.

Lecture 04.1 Version 02

Ken Modd's own understanding of being a father was a result of the conditioning he created; contrary to what his childhood provided him. What he learned from his own life as a child were the elements of physical, emotional, sexual, and verbal violence.

When Modd's first child arrived, he had already made a transparent and unshakable conviction to himself; long before. Such conviction was that he would never 'put his hand' on his children. This is a man whose complete childhood was deranged and robbed of him, and whose vision of the past is severally limited to the horror that occurred as a child. The ability to alter the existence of such violence and overlook the scars, for the purpose of not giving his own child a comparable life, is striking. And it is the man himself, Kenneth James Modd, which I commend with sincere gratitude for having raised children without touching them in a violent way.

As the physical element of violence is the worst, it is usually the most difficult for a person to alleviate from his or her own way of life, and while the absence of physical violence is a good and necessary thing, considering his conditioned life, the other side to Modd's story is unfortunate, though.

Physical violence was not the only single act in the play of his youth. This idea of never spanking his own children came to Modd in the middle of a beating. After several strikes he began to tolerate the pain, and shortly thereafter, he unrecognized the pain. He now lived in a very short and brief time span where analysis and dissection began to take place.

Surely he did not recognize theory such as 'cause and effect' as he had not been administered such scientific terminology yet in his education. But there was analysis ongoing in his fragile mind; somewhere along the way an admonishment entered his young, analytic psyche. He recalled many days in his own backyard, when he heard the laughter and shouting at the birthday parties. Modd recalled the times when his hateful family took him to the public pool, where all the children went with their parents. The simple logic that children and their families should be together and laugh together, and the logic that children are the most important thing of all to a mother and father, and other similar logic, were the driving factors that lead to this unrelenting conviction of Modd's.

He would never strike his own children; he received this message through a beating. The beatings were his teacher.

The other acts of violence in his childhood were emotional and verbal. The unfortunate duality I eluded to earlier lie herein-he never pursued study on the subjects of emotional and verbal abuse.

How was he supposed to know that his duty, his responsibility, was to sit with a young child and teach her to give thanks, and have pride, and a vision? How was he to know that he was supposed to be there for her at every turn? Why was it so special to bring a child to school? To attend all the school functions? How could a man with no conditioning as a father and much violent conditioning as a son understand the roles and responsibilities of a father? It is inconceivable to believe that such a hand-off to fatherhood, without the right tools, could yield positive results.

When a man is running as a result of fear, it is hard for him to take care of his own self; in his unconscious mind, it is even more difficult to take care of a child. He knows that he is ill equipped to handle such task. He tells himself how weak he is. And it is this very knowledge that makes him run. But, where is the knowledge coming from?

He didn't spend his life thinking about how to raise a child from the moment he left home as a young boy to the day he stood in the hospital room staring at his newborn. How was he to know that this precious gift would have to be loved and nurtured and taught the ways of the world?

The conditioning of his life will always haunt him. Even now, as the children become adult themselves, there is uncertainty in the relationship he seeks to recover. While there is now an understanding of such violent conditioning derived from his childhood, Modd's intuition continues to rally the call of fear. The fear now, though, is fear of the loss of a relationship with the grown children, or their inability to gain trust in him. He fears that they will never truly understand the reason for his running; for his fear. And until they do, such anguish will continue to thrive.

VI.

28th of March

It has not always been like this, oh book, this wretchedness, this squalor. I held a heavy workload at the University; not too heavy always, but gruesome only at times. I lectured twice a week and gave tests. The routine became stagnant after a few years and that is when I became compelled to put books together. One particular year, on the first day of the semester-it was raining and miserable-I showed up drunk. Nobody except me knew I was drunk in front of a class of incoming freshmen. They listened with heightened anticipation, paying no attention to my stupor or misdeeds. I played it off as well as I could, almost stumbling across the desk at some point, and I was strict in my demands when I spoke. It was the only time I showed up fully punch-drunk and I gave much thought to the potential ramifications of such actions thereafter.

As the years passed by, I developed a heightened enthusiasm for writing books; the pay and fringe benefits became more important than anything else at the University and soon boredom challenged me more than the lesson plans and lectures. I had no superiors except for the Dean, and he spent more time on vacations, using days he had built up over a forty-seven year career. So, as it may, it became a redundant world where I simply "cut and paste" or personalized the previous years lesson plans and tests into the present years work plan; I lectured less and less and depended more on the students to fulfill their own educational needs. And of course, oh book, there was always one or two students that were exceptionally gifted and demanded my time.

After a typical day at the school I slipped into my old blue Volvo and drove the hour and a half home; not a day passed where that hour and a half wouldn't be filled with thoughts of writing books. It weighed on me heavily. I began to spend less time engulfed in the schoolwork and more time searching for the information I needed for the future novels that I so dreamed of creating. I found myself, as I sat at my desk in the lecture hall in front of sixty-two students, reviewing and doing edit work to one of the books that I was about to hand off to my publisher. I had to reach my senses and realize that my own mind could not successfully do both of these chores simultaneously and so I began to awaken in the middle of the night to write. At least I could leave the writing at home and fully concentrate on my professorship and the needs of the students. That was when I hired the young Arab to drive me and slept on the ride.

The first book "The Conditioning of a Man" was the hardest to put together. There were many times where a long span prevailed prior to the next writing; it became so challenging that I almost gave up; neither the words nor the storyline came easy and I put so much resistance to my thoughts. I tried to manage every single word and sentence. I tried to be proficient in every word structure; I realized at some point that I was fighting a losing battle. I just couldn't keep it easy and allow the words to flow. The whiskey helped. The pills helped.

After three years and three published books I set the pencils down and did not write again for four years. I do not recall, dear book, the reason why my lust and passion for writing had changed. I think this most probably was the time that I became introduced to heroin.

As my second wife had died of an aneurism and I lived alone in my redbrick two-story home, I began to use up the personal and vacation days due to me from the University. For almost four years I was able to stay away from the campus for about ten months at a time. This was when the inspiration I needed arrived and I developed and wrote my most successful work "The Distance Between Fenceposts". Locked in the dark house alone and quiet, like a hermit, the internal guide that I relied on so heavily for the thoughts lead me in a certain direction. I tried as best as I could to keep my 'self' out of the equation and allowed the mind to put it all together.

And so, it was a mind, filled with whiskey and heroin, which assisted me in creating this masterpiece in which I won so many accolades for. Barely eating, I lost weight during this period. While consumed in it all, I overlooked the care that my own body needed and became sick on a few occasions. When my health became better I decided to take up walking and each time I attempted to, as I was merely a half mile down the road, I would turn around and rush back to the writing, as something new and very important had entered my thoughts and desperately needed to be written down; I was seemingly forgetting things at that point. And I gave little thought to that, too.

When I showed up in New York at the award ceremony from the Writer's Guild, like all the other writer's there, I was skinny like a broom and hopped up on booze and heroin. Oh book, it was a happy time in my life-a successful time. The folded up napkin in which I wrote my speech reads, "It has been a long struggle to reach this destination. At first I stumbled and fell; then I got up and brushed myself off. I stayed on the same path and fell again; again I got up. I stayed on the same path and slipped a little. Then, unknowingly, I took a different path and the final walk got me here. Along this particular path I passed two signs. One read ALLOW and the other read ACCEPT."

When the concept of allowing the words to come in, no matter what the prolific and gurgled mind wanted, and to accept the mere fact that the words arrived, all began to occur, telling the story became the journey itself. I surrendered to it all.

27th of March

Lecture 08 Version 02

As babies we learn sound. As we grow, we learn that there are, indeed, different sounds. At some point later we learn to differentiate those sounds. And, at a much later time we learn words, then sentences, and so forth. This is the basic chain to verbal communication; though there is even more taking place way before that, in the womb.

My aim here is to identify the misunderstood value of language. Language is the driving factor in the success or failure of humans in their species. History has shown that, as man has been able to communicate more affectively, overall, as a society, there is less effort for him to kill another, although it still exists. So, the inevitability of such avocation is that the language we are conditioned with drives our future. It has driven the past, but cannot drive the present moment, as all that exists in the present moment is stillness.

For Ken Modd, a boy that stepped away from the inhumane childhood, this has been tantamount to torture for him; an unsuccessful ability to use language in a way where others aren't directly affected or hurt. The verbal violence of his childhood-the name calling and yelling of profanities-has prohibited Modd from achieving success in his personal relationships, and even in his work relationships, yet, this too, he has been unaware of to the point where something different had to be tried; some other road taken. The unawareness is the culprit.

This conditioning of violence in language is understood little by most societies. The need to call another by a name different than his or her own, in a negative connotation is not truly what that person is; it more so describes who the one is calling the name, and the type of person he is. It is the way the name-caller thinks, by his very own conditioning.

Lecture 08.12 Version 02

In almost all cases where there is physical and verbal violence in a household, there exists sexual violence; these components of violence are usually linked together, dependent on each other. There was nothing horrific that happened to Ken on a sexual level; his writing has given me no indication of such.

As a whole, however, the acts of the family-such behavior-are an indication that sexual violence deeply affected the young boy, and has full ramifications on his life. This conditioning that I endeavor to explain had its fare share in the actions Ken Modd has taken in his marital life; my assessment clearly indicates that, had he been conscious of-aware of-and knowledgeable of such behavior that was so vile and vehement, Ken would have been able to communicate better with his partners.

A young Ken learned to misidentify quickly with events; he rapidly learned to "see nothing and know nothing". As naked men walked through his open room to reach the shotgun houses only bathroom, if he were in bed, Modd would close his eyes and pretend to be sleeping as the naked body opened the adjourning door next to Aunt Mildred's room. If he were playing in the middle of the day with his plastic G.I. Joe toys, he would just continue playing as though nothing ever happened. He knew what the outcome would be if he paid attention to any of it; he associated pain to such knowledge.

As time passed, and he gained confidence, he began to closely stare at each man, one by one, careful not to get caught. The room was very small so everything was close to everything else, even naked men walking swiftly through a young boys room.

The young Modd turned the grossness of the situation into a game at some point. On a white paper, hidden between the wood planks in his closet, he would draw a stick figure that resembled each man in some way. He began measuring by eye, and imagination, the size of the testicle sack on each man. Then he would compose what he felt was the appropriate size to the stick figure. He learned to move the pain away, and add something else in its place. This was an unknown path into the world of meditation.

There is a danger to a child's life to be witness to sexual acts between one's own family and strangers. Not only did the young boy see strange, unknown naked men trampling through the home he lived in, with the only family he knew. Ken, as a curious adolescent put his innocent eyes through the keyhole, curious of what was happening in the next room as he heard cries and pants. If he got away with it once, he told himself, then he would do it again, and again. He first saw it and felt something very wrong; it shocked him. It scared him. The first time it scared him so much; in fact, he almost screamed. But he thought quickly of the consequences to follow should he yell. And the second time he did it was because he felt only minimal pain from the first look; not enough to bar him from doing it again; and, consequently, each time he did it thereafter-peeked through the keyhole-he was examining, studying, and learning. Most importantly, unconsciously, he was conditioning himself by such surroundings.

Modd's Uncle would remain for weeks away at a time with his work. The other men came. The other men left. Some stayed for the weekend. There would be drinking and drugging and sexual activity. When some became bored they turned on the video player and inserted one of the many porno tapes that rested freely on the shelf. These films weren't of women dancing with poles or strip teases; no, they were the raunchiest filth available in pornography.

Sometimes the porn stayed on for hours, continuously replaying itself while the men masturbated or fell asleep or left the home to get more booze or drugs. It was very convenient for the six-year-old kid to jump into the recliner and gain such education.

The spontaneous episodes of naked men running through his room, watching the sexual activity through the door's keyhole, and the timeless volume of pornography watched through several years of a young child's life generates a devastating conditioning.

This form of sexual violence taught Ken the negative side, the complete opposite, of the way life truly is supposed to be in monogamous relationships. It has a tremendous impact on a young adult male just beginning to reach out to women.

This conditioned way taught Modd to have lust in his mind. At first instance of the sight of a woman his mind automatically begins to judge. His brutal memory, this pain-corpse, merged along the way his memory with the physical attributes of the women in the porn films. As female after female after female appeared in these movies, they all had the same things in common. And it is these commonalities that would develop into a singular image of a woman. They would be tall with big breasts, a large butt, and puffy lips. Such image would become a prototype in Modd's mind as he merged the conditioned pain of the sexual violence with the beauty of the woman's figure. They would become one, and would remain being the underlying, hidden pain-corpse.

As long as he did not comprehend fully what affect such conditioned mind was actually having on his relationships, Modd could not make any changes to this behavior that seemed to be recurring with each different relationship. He did not give in to the notion that it was simply not a just thing to lust over a beautiful woman. The drinking buddies and acquaintances of his felt a similar way, but they, too, live with a futile mind born from conditioning, and their aberrant behavior was no teacher to Modd.

Whether he knew it or not, the pornography was a teacher in many ways to the young Ken Modd. Negatively, it taught him to use lust to satisfy the mind, to ease it, if only temporarily. It became what was to be the main ingredient for his failed relationships, having a 'grass is greener on the other side' mentality.

The porno's never showed the woman to be caring, religious, or faithful. Modd's impression of women continued to be held hostage to the images in the films. Such images are in direct correlation with the pain-corpse, each depend on the other for fuel. Until Modd fully comprehends that this image of a woman needs to be altered-it needs to become something entirely new and different-then this conditioning will control his life. While caring and faithful women never appeared in the pornography, such ideals weren't present in the home, either.

The thesis has all been completed, reader. Barron has placed an unimaginable amount of time into the readings and has studied it with great contemplation. He has done so under the futile conditions of alcoholism, drug addiction, and an impaired memory.

As you have read, it is clear that the humanoid can survive without a memory. The capitulating mind of man, through tribal conditioning, gives in to legend that memory is vital for the heart to beat, the kidney to function, the brain to work, and the form of a humanoid to exist. It is farthest from the truth; memory only contains the past and a desire to be somewhere else (the future).

-Page 01-

I do not really know where to start. I feel, somewhere inside, that I have been a man of literary pursuit as I have constantly dreamt of composing words each day since the elderly lady picked me up from the ditch next to the road and I've been able to get back a little strength. She brought me here to her home-a lovely and warm home-and allowed me to stay in a room. From time to time she comes in and offers a warm bowl of soup and gives me a sponge bath, as I am too weak to do it myself. The soup has little meat and is bare, but I am trembling and pale and the holes in my arm bleed.

She told me that today was two days before Christmas. I have stared at these walls filled with black and white photos of strangers and small wooden shelves with knick-knacks that fall off when the train passes.

I asked her for sheets of paper to write on. She handed me an aged yellow pad with dust on it. Perhaps I can begin to put together some missing pieces that I, undoubtedly, am not seeing clearly now.

There was a fire. I don't remember it; I just remember waking up on the ground next to the burned outline of a building next to an old rusty ladder. The outline of the burned charcoal represented the footprint of the building. It was a mere pile, about two inches high, of black dust and coal and looked spectacular, as if some child had poured it in a straight line from a bottle. I gather it was my place, but I am not sure. I have no wallet or identification; the fact of the matter is I have no memory of my own name.

I walked around the burned building in search of anything I could call my own. The only thing that was not totally charred was this old book that I now have resting on top of the chifforobe. It's front and rear covers are too burned to be recognized, as is about ninety percent of its contents. The few pages that remain may provide some insight to my life, as it seems my memory has failed and I cannot recall many basic things. I have so many questions that need answers to and perhaps I can put it all together with the help of the charred remaining's of these writings.

-Page 02-

I gently and methodically separated the pages from each other, being careful not to tear more than what was already. I wasn't successful in doing so, as the waterlogged book had become cemented together. Some words are clear; most I am unable to decipher. I hoped to find a name, maybe an address; even some general happening that I could relate to. It was clear that I was waging a thwarted effort and would have little to calculate from.

The old lady asked what I was doing. After I told her she left the room abruptly, only to walk back in two minutes later with a large hand-held magnifying glass. I thanked her and she removed herself from my pressing work and the room.

I turned page after page of the large burned book. Just when it seemed that my patience had reached its end, I found the first page of legible writing. As the book is exceedingly brittle, I handled it with care and have written the words here in the event I am unable to read it again because of its fragility. The first text I read is as such:

"She shoved her huge, white-skinned fat knee against my small head as I knelt on my knees with my face pressed in the corner. My small head was jammed in between the knee that was pushed forward with all of her body weight-all three hundred pounds-and one of the three brass hinges that supported the small closet door. Once she backed off a little, my body slipped downward to the floor, following the contour of the corner in front of me; the hollow impression formed in my head left from the brass hinge remained there four or five minutes until returning to its original state. She then stomped on my head with her large shoeless feet, and as I covered the head with my six-year-old hands and arms, giving it some protection, she worked on the body downward to the stomach, where she stomped the big fat feet and rapidly kicked there."

I found it impossible to swallow and to breathe after reading such words. I did not allow myself to pause for too long and I hastily opened the broken book to another page that had a few legible words remaining:

"I put two shells in the Iraqi soldier, both right at his mid-section. The four warning shots just were of no meaning to him as he barged towards me and, essentially, committed suicide. I was broke, too, so I took his wallet."

Without any additional thought, I placed the remnants of the book back into the tall, worn chifforobe, closed its doors, and walked to the kitchen to have some tea. Sensing that I was grief-stricken, and after I told her that I have no memory of my mother, the old lady served my tea, smiled, and told me, in her own effort to be kind, "never forget where you come from." It was a nice gesture.

To read such passages from my own diary, not even recognizing my own language or handwriting, brings suffering. My mind is racing and the thoughts are scattered; there is imbalance and chaos that I cannot recognize.

There is much instability associated with not knowing who you are. I am not sure if I should meditate or pray.

ACKNOWLEDGEMENTS

To the many of you that have sought an understanding of the world through my eyes, my experience, and my writings, I thank you. Continue to knock on my door; continue to find me.

The much anticipated Volume II
of the _Lemons on a Plate_ series by

Pat Black

"The Distance between Fenceposts"

Visit

www.lemonsonaplate.com

www.ingramcontent.com/pod-product-compliance
Lightning Source LLC
Chambersburg PA
CBHW030516260626
47157CB00005B/1761